DRAGON'S MATE

RED PLANET DRAGONS OF TAJSS BOOK TWO

MIRANDA MARTIN

CONTENTS

Like being stranded on a desert alien planet wasn't enough...

All I ever wanted was someone to love. Now my best friend is knocked up by the only hunky alien-dragon available and I can't tell anyone how totally jealous I am. The handful of humans who survived our ship's crash are locked in a struggle to live in sweltering heat with dwindling supplies.

The others are taking the life giving, addictive epis but if I take it that means I'm stuck here. Forever. Which also means the chance of being rescued by a knight in shining armor would be zero.

If that weren't enough, I go and get myself kidnapped and he's another big, sexy, alien-dragon warrior.

SVERRE

I slide to a stop. My internal alarms are going off. The sand sinks as my wings fold tight against my back. I lash my tail back and forth, keeping myself balanced. From this cliff, I can see one of the old cities in the distance. I can feel the demarcation. I'm about to cross into another's territory. This is wrong. I shouldn't do this. It will lead to a confrontation.

Crouching down, I bury my hands in the hot, red sand. A breeze shifts the lines of the sand dunes across the distance. The shades of red vary from so light as to appear almost white to a deep maroon. Massive rocks dot the landscape as well. This is rough terrain, not conducive to fast travel and with too many hiding places for predators. And it's another Zmaj's territory.

I remember before. Before the attacks, before my failure, when our home was the center of the galaxy. Before this territorial urge that rules us. Before, when things were right. Shaking my head, I push away those memories. They are the past. The past doesn't matter. Now matters. Now I must know what fell from the sky. The flash and the streak that brought back my hazy memories. It might be hope.

A herd of bivo travels below me, moving slow. They are large herd animals and seeing them makes my stomach rumble. I could hunt and take one, which would give me plenty of extra food for this journey, but I'm sure I'm not the only one who saw the flash and streak across the sky. Anyone else could be on their way. I have to see what fell myself. I have to know first before I let any others scavenge. If it is visitors from off our planet, I'm the best one to find them. The others are too far gone into bijass, the regression. They didn't believe me when I told them it would happen after the devastation. They laughed, but I was right. We've regressed back to our primitive roots.

After the devastation there were so few of us left that we gathered together. No females survived, and it was apparent we were at the end of our race. I told them then, argued, that we should stay together. Work together to find a way off the planet, to find if any of the other races survived the war. Most laughed at me then, but I knew. I knew what would happen, and it has. Primal instincts, the territorial nature of our species, the desire for treasures, and the urge to fight for dominance have taken over since we've all been alone for so long. I had a few supporters but I've long since lost any contact.

I run along the ridge, following as it slopes down. My wings spread and give me enough lift that I can run lightly across the sand that would otherwise slow me down. Using my tail, I keep my balance and move quickly. When the cliff is low enough, I jump off the side and use my wings to glide and land in a crouch.

I look around to make sure there are no threats then run forward. As I cross the line into another's territory, my skin tingles and my guts tighten. A voice in my head screams at me as instinct urges me to turn back. I can't though. I have to know, so I run. I run for all I'm worth, while keeping my senses alert to all possible threats. This far out from the city, I shouldn't raise alarms with the territory's owner. Likely, he's heading for the same goal I am.

A massive, standing ridge comes closer as I run. Hopefully from that rise I'll be able to see my goal. The ground rumbles underneath my feet and I freeze in place. Damn it, I don't have time for this but it might be a zemlja. Monster worms that dig their way through the earth, the most dangerous thing on the planet. They hunt by sound and vibration. I hold completely still, waiting until the rumble of its passage fades.

Satisfied, I stand and resume running. The ridge is close, I'm almost to its shadow when the ground rumbles again but this time it's too late. I'm in trouble. I unsheathe my lochaber, spread my wings and leap into the air. Catching the wind, I drift until I'm over a boulder fallen from the ridge. Closing my wings, I land lightly on the rock then hold my breath, unmoving.

The ground trembles, sand shifts, then bounces. The creature is directly below and massive based on how much the sand is shifting. They rarely enter my territory so my memory of them is faded, my instinct for dealing with them rusty. I should have sensed its closeness long before I did. The tremors slow then fade to a stop as it passes by. Watching the sand stop shifting I can guess that it's moving away. Good. One man alone doesn't stand a chance against a zemlja.

I wait longer, unwilling to risk attracting its attention because I wasn't patient. Patience is a virtue I've long practiced. If only I'd had it before the devastation. Memories sift through the fog of time, trying to come back to the fore but I have no time. Turning on the boulder to look up the ridge behind me, I think I can make it if I leap. I tense the muscles of my legs and relax them, preparing for the jump.

I push off, spreading my wings to gain height. The strain pulls at the muscles of my shoulders and back as I cross the distance. Reaching for the ridge, I'm almost to it when I start dropping. Damn it! Pushing my wings harder, I fight, using them against their intended purpose of gliding. Zmaj are not sismis, we do not fly but I try. Gravity pulls hard and I drop faster. Stretching my arm out, I catch a crack in the ridge. Sharp edges dig into the soft skin of my fingers as I'm jerked towards the ground.

"Ugh," I grunt as I slam against the ragged edges.

My scales protect me from most of the impact but my clothes are worse for the wear. Hanging by one arm, my muscles scream in pain at the abuse. Scrabbling my feet, I finally find purchase that lets me take the pressure off my arm. I spot a crack just over my head that I can put my other hand into and then I start working my way up the face of the cliff. Moving one hand at a time, I pull up until I find footing then gain a few more precious inches.

I'm almost to the top. Reaching for the next crack, I'm about to grab it when something darts out so fast I barely register the motion. I pull my hand back, narrowly avoiding being bitten by the zmeya. That was close. The venom of a zmeya is highly poisonous, causing paralysis, which allows it to drain the blood from its victim.

Using my now free hand, I dig into my pouch and pull out a stick. Shifting my feet, I find a solid purchase point so that I can stand and free both my hands. Knife in one hand and stick in the other, I tap the stick up the wall below the crack the zmeya is hiding in. As the stick crests the opening the snake strikes, digging its fangs in. I pull the stick back and bring the knife down behind it, severing the thing's head from its body.

I tap the wall a few more times to make sure there are no more hiding then drop the stick and resume my climb. In moments, I'm on top of the ridge and closing my outer lids to shield my eyes from the sun. Smoke climbs towards the sky on the horizon. Good, I'm getting closer. I adjust my gear until I'm more comfortable then start running. The sun is getting low, which means I'll have to stop for the night before I reach my goal. Being exposed at night is foolish and I won't risk it, even for the hope of arriving first.

When I hear the first sismis cry, I know I have to stop. The creatures are flying vampires and hunt the dark in swarms.

I drop to the ground and shift from side to side, digging my body into the sand until I'm mostly buried. The covering of sand is enough protection so I can doze to pass the time.

I'm awakened by a herd of bivo passing below. My stomach grumbles and the urge for fresh meat is almost enough to pull me from my rest but then I hear a hiss. I wait, sure I know what's about to happen and I'm not wrong. Three guster leap on the alpha bivo's back. The bivo screams a high pitched, ear splitting sound that tears through the night as the guster lock their jaws. The bivo's massive, fur covered head swings side to side but its protruding tusks can't find purchase on the attackers who have hit it from behind.

It stumbles and falls to the ground as the herd stampedes away, leaving him to his fate. The guster tear it apart, feeding in a frenzy. It's not long before there's nothing left but bones that the guster lick clean before returning to the hunt for their next meal. The rest of the night passes uneventfully except for a clutch of sismis flying overhead, but they don't stay around for long.

As the sun crests the horizon and the sand warms, I wake and rise, shaking myself free. I resume my run, knowing I still have a long way to go. I fall into a rhythm that passes the miles and the time. One step, two, one step, two. A steady pace that beats down the distance through consistent forward motion. I have to go around large rocks and, as I get closer, massive dunes block my vision until I reach the top of the tallest ones. The terrain here is completely different from home. The dunes are all soft sand. Home is surrounded by ridges, rocks, broken remains of the ancient mountains and the ground is much rougher.

Climbing to the top of yet another dune, I spy my goal in the distance. It's massive and out of place sitting on the horizon. An enormous steel structure jutting into the sky. Smoke drifts from its jagged edges and debris dots the surrounding fields. When I close my protective lenses, my vision becomes clearer and I can see tiny figures moving. Off-worlders. It has to be. There aren't that many Zmaj left on the entire planet and they'd be trying to kill each other if gathered in the same place.

The sun is low again before I get within sight of my target. I stop and rest again for the night. Tomorrow, I will reach my goal. It has to be fast enough. Has to be. The future of my race depends on it. I don't sleep. My thoughts run in an eternal circle that won't let me rest. Memories keep threatening to emerge from the fog of time but I don't look at them. I don't want to remember. There's pain hidden inside there and I know it. Terrible things happened back then and I remember enough to work towards the future without having to know more.

As the sun climbs back into the sky, I emerge from the sand and make my final run. Reaching the top of a dune, I drop to the ground then crawl forward. There are dozens of alien, strange looking people marching away in a line. At the head of the line stand three people and one of them is a Zmaj. His eyes scan the dunes and I'm certain this is his territory. Instinct roars up at the sight of him and I quiver with the urge to race down the dune and challenge him for the aliens.

That is not my purpose. I'm better than that. We're better than that—or we can be. I struggle with the instinctive drive until, at last, my head clears and I can observe. The aliens are shockingly different and clearly unsuited for life on Tajss. Their faces and hands don't show any scales. Almost all of them are a bright red color that doesn't look healthy. They stumble as they walk and some of them are having to help or carry others.

I camouflage myself and then track the line as they march. One of them swings its arms and looks as if it bounces with each step. It's shorter than most of the others and stays close to the first three I saw. Something about it, even at this distance, makes me think female. I can't see her clearly but I hear her voice and that sound calls to me. It's light and filled with joy. Listening to it creates a tingle that runs through my limbs into my core. Suddenly my prime penis is erect and pressing painfully against my pants. I want her. I have to have her.

Control. I have to stay in control, keep my head clear. I can't let the other see me. If the other Zmaj becomes aware of my presence, it will lead to a fight. That is not what I want. I have to know more. How did the others come to be here?

Her voice drifts across the sand and I smile. I have to see the person from which such a beautiful sound comes. The aliens stumble along behind the Zmaj, making slow progress. They aren't dealing well with the environment here on this planet. The heat is sapping their strength and their design is poor for traveling across the loose sand. I track alongside them, being careful to remain out of sight.

They stop at night and make camps. They don't camouflage themselves. They don't even try. Many of them just drop where they stop. Stupid and dangerous. I can't believe the Zmaj allows it, but he stays at the lead, only letting two of them near him. The one with the musical voice stays a short distance back so I work my way closer. She's sitting next to a small fire and talking in her sweet, beautiful voice to three others. They all look like females as well.

I'm close enough to catch hints of her smell when the wind shifts. Sweet, musky, with hints of a spice. It's intoxicating. Her face is perfect if lacking in proper, protective scales. She's shorter than the other aliens. The fur on her head is dark, draping around her face and reaching her shoulders. Her skin has the same red tone as the others but not as deep, more golden. Her eyes are shaped like nuts from the baoba tree. She smiles, showing teeth that aren't sharp. Do they not eat meat?

She rises to her feet and walks around the others, stooping and helping each of them to have a drink. She talks, a lot, and I listen to the sound of her while drifting towards sleep. I'll stay close. If anything comes and threatens her, I'll be here.

Sounds awake me with a start. The sun is rising.

The sound again breaks the quiet, red morning. It's loud and almost raucous. I resist the urge to jump to my feet while looking for its source. I can't reveal my presence here unless it's unavoidable. Three of the aliens are in a circle, including the one with the music in her voice. She is making gestures and sounds then the three of them make the same raucous sound again, shaking their heads and holding their sides. Strange, perhaps it's a morning ritual of theirs?

The Zmaj storms through, barking orders and yelling for

them to hurry as another day begins. I trail them for two days before I'm sure of their destination and my heart sinks seeing it on the horizon. He's taking them to his city. He's claiming them all for himself. The urge to fight rages but I would lose. I've seen him now. He's a warrior where I was never bred for such. I can fight, I can defend myself and mine, but against a warrior the outcome is far from sure. If I have time to plan, set traps, I would win. In straight, mindless, toe-to-toe combat, I'm not sure I would.

Patience, I hiss softly. Patience and I will gain what I want. I trail them and watch her. She will be mine. It's been a long time since I acquired a new treasure. She is the perfect one. I want to listen to the musical sound of her voice for all time.

Eventually I track them until they reach the ruins of an ancient city. It's been a long time since I've seen one of the old cities. The fact that the owner has held on to it is a testament to his power as a warrior. I'm sure he's had more than one challenger over the years. I wonder if any of the old tech is still working. I'd love an opportunity to explore the city, to see what is working, what remains from before, but I can't risk it. If I set foot inside, it will be a direct affront to his territory. If he's slid too far into the bijass there will be no reasoning with him.

I wait. Hoping. What else do I have? I can't get the sound of her voice out of my mind. It echoes through my memory, calling to me, telling me to save her. Make her mine. Even the bijass works against me on this, since it makes me want her to be my treasure. It pushes me to claim her. Wisdom keeps me outside the city but my drive is to storm in and take what I want. Stupid idea. I don't deserve to have beautiful things such as her. I'm unworthy of any reward, no treasures can be mine, the inner voice whispers but I ignore that.

That voice speaks from the fog of the past and is not to be trusted.

Another night passes. My scales itch because I'm in another's territory. I want to fight or leave but those primal urges don't control me. I'm not lost yet. I am in control of myself and my mind, so I stay and wait.

2

JOLIE

*F*our weeks. It's been four weeks since life was turned upside down. Four hot, long, dry weeks since the only home I ever knew crash landed on this forsaken desert hell.

Stupid space pirates.

Seriously, can't they find anything better to do than attack generational colony ships?

But anyway, here we are. That's the beauty of being human; we survive, even on a planet like this. Those who care finally settled on calling it Vulcan. The war between Star Trek and Star Wars continues but, apparently, more Trekkies survived the crash than Star Wars fans.

It's hot, so damn hot. I grab a bottle of water and down it.

"You know," I say to Calista as I return to studying a sample of local vegetation through a microscope. "This place really looks like Gallifrey."

I wait for her response, adjusting the magnification, but Calista doesn't answer.

"Gallifrey, especially if we get the dome working," I repeat.

"I kn-" she says, but then she's running for a bucket.

I jump up, grab some scraps of cloth, and do what any BFF does. I hold her hair back and make soothing noises while she hurls. When she's done, I hand her the cloth, and she wipes her mouth. She's pale and there's sweat on her brow and lip.

"Are you okay?" I ask.

"Um, yeah, I think so," she says. "Maybe something I ate."

I look at her carefully, trying to see if she's really okay. We're on a strange planet eating foreign food with god knows what microbes and bacteria. Having digestive problems would be no surprise but, as I look my friend over, I notice something else. Is she bloated? Calista is the savior of our people, more or less. After we crashed, she was out looking for edible vegetation when she was kidnapped by one of the indigenous aliens, Ladon. Alien but humanoid enough to be compatible, because the two of them fell for each other, hard.

How can she be the one that gets so lucky? On the ship, there were thousands of potential mates. All of them human, too. Now that we've crashed on a devastated planet only a small percentage of us seem to have survived.. The selection of eligible bachelors went from really great to non-existent. None of the men who survived are my knight in shining armor.

She's a beautiful girl, totally sexy nerd chic. We've been best friends since I can remember and I love her dearly but I can admit, if only to myself, that I'm envious. I always thought I'd be the one to settle down first. Calista wasn't the dating type and rarely took an interest in men.

"What?" she asks as I continue looking her over.

"Nothing," I say, turning away. "So yeah, Gallifrey, you know, Doctor Who?"

"You're not getting off that easy. What?"

"Nothing, seriously."

"It's not nothing, and it's not Doctor Who. What is it?"

"Well, it's just…" I trail off and try to come up with some way of getting out of the hole I've dug. "Have you put on some weight?"

"What? No! I mean, no!" Her face flushes and I'm in deep. Her hands go to her stomach and flatten against it. "Maybe I'm a little bloated."

"Um huh," I say, not taking my attention off the microscope.

"Okay, give, what?" she asks again.

"It's just… look- I'm just asking, but when did you last have your period?"

"My what? Um," she purses her lips, thinking, "before the crash."

"Which was almost a month ago by ship time."

"No, that can't be, I mean, it's just stress right? All the stress of living here, surviving. Pressure can do that to a girl."

"Sure, it could be," I agree. "Do you think that's all it is?"

"It has to be! I mean, the only guy I've been with is Ladon and…" she trails off.

"Uh-huh," I say and smile my best, reassuring smile.

"Oh my god," she says, her voice dropping to a whisper. She grabs the chair next to me for support, but then plops down in it.

I take her hands in mine. "Yes! This is so exciting!"

"No, it's not," she says and I can see the fear in her eyes. "I don't know… what if… how does his race…"

"Bah! We'll figure it out. You're brilliant and so am I. Cross that bridge when we get there."

"Easy for you to say," she whispers, tears welling in her eyes, so I pull her into a tight hug.

"It's fine," I say softly while stroking her hair. "We got this."

"Yeah, it's just, scary you know?"

"Yeah, sure, but it'll be okay. We got this. Besides, he dotes on you! Hell, I'm jealous. I want a guy who looks at me like he does you."

"Yeah, he does, doesn't he?" she says, smiling at last.

"Hell yes! He's over the moon for you and you know it. You see the way his eyes light up as soon as he sees you?"

"I've got to tell him!" she says.

"Yes you do!" I say in my most enthusiastic voice. She hugs me tight then runs off, leaving me alone.

Slumping into my chair, I sigh. It's not fair. The empty ache in my core yawns, threatening to swallow me whole. I want what she has so much but now I'm here. On this planet with a handful of survivors. The odds of finding what I want are astronomical, twenty four point two trillion to one to be exact. The odds that a rescue ship will arrive in my lifetime. So yeah, this sucks. Yet, I'm happy for her. Jealous, yes, but happy. I can be both, right? Sure I can. I'm doing it right now.

I need to get my mind off this and onto something else. Anything else. I'll go back to the barracks. Maybe some of the other girls will be there. That will cheer me up. I kill the power to the lab and walk out. Our energy generation is limited and can't be wasted. Hopefully Amara is making headway on that problem. And the dome, the dome is most important of all I guess.

We got lucky, depending on how you look at things. If we had to crash land on an alien planet that was not our destination, at least it's one that isn't filled with hostile aliens. Snorting, I laugh out loud. This planet is hostile but the only intelligent alien we've met is nice. Sexy, hot, big and massively manly in every way possible. I can only imagine how good he is in bed. But he's taken. So taken.

The rest of the planet has been working to kill us off as fast as possible. Like we're an invading bacteria that it wants cleansed from itself. Heat, unbearable heat, animals that kill anything and everything, and even the damn plants are likely to kill you.

Yeah, this place is rough. That's why we have to get the shields up on this ruin of a city. It will lock out the roaming monsters. Two people were killed yesterday by a pack of guster. Nasty pack creatures that seem to be the top of the local food chain. A guster is a large, razor-toothed reptile with four legs, wide webbed feet and hulking mounds across its back. Spines stick out at various points along the hard leather skin to help ward off any predators. Super scary, thinking about them makes me shudder.

Before I leave the lab building, I take time at the door to stare around carefully and make sure it's safe to exit. The sun is low, and the buildings cast long shadows across empty, ruined streets. When I step outside, sweat instantly starts to pour down my face. It's so damn hot here. My mouth and throat go dry, but I don't want to take time to drink so I run down the street towards the barracks. This city was probably beautiful once, decades ago, before the planet was devastated. The skyscrapers show decay. The material the road was made of has pockmarks and plants are growing in every crack. Slowly Nature is reclaiming what's hers. Red sand drifts through the streets and heat assaults everything.

Calista found videos that tell the history of this place. It was once a thriving galaxy with highly advanced technology. This planet, Tajss as Ladon calls it, is the only place that epis grows. Epis is a local plant that has amazing traits including the extension of life. It changes you when you take it on a cellular level. Eventually, a war broke out among the planets of this galaxy, apparently over epis, and in the end the planet was bombed and almost all life was destroyed.

Ladon survived. He says, according to Calista since she's the only one who can talk to him, that there are others. All this happened many decades ago. Maybe more, Ladon doesn't remember very well.

I reach the barracks without incident and step out of the heat into the cool darkness with great relief. After a long drink from my water bottle, I head towards the sound of voices. When I enter the dining room several of my friends are gathered around the table, eating.

"Jolie!" Inga says, smiling.

Inga is looking better now that we've gotten shelter from the direct sun. Her fair skin and red hair isn't burnt like it was. Her smile is bright and cheery. There's a quiet toughness to her despite what she's gone through.

"Hey," I say, returning her smile.

Mei and Amara wave and greet me around mouthfuls of food.

"Anyone else here?" I ask, grabbing a plate and helping myself.

"Not yet," Mei says.

Mei is so beautiful it hurts. When she's in the room, it makes me feel plain and boring. Her beauty is so easy. Even here in our rough surroundings, crashed on an alien planet, she still looks perfect. Her white gold hair has body and shine, her skin is flawless, her eyes are bright and her teeth are perfect. Gah, if she wasn't so nice I'd have to contemplate killing her. Kidding! But she is just too much to take sometimes.

"How's the generator project, Amara?" I ask.

"Shit," she says, swallowing. "Absolute, total shit."

"What's wrong with them?"

"You mean besides the fact that they've sat unused for forever? They're locked up. I'm going to have to tear them apart, clean each part, then hope to hell I can put them back together correctly. The technology is different from ours by far and I'm not familiar with most of it."

"That sounds not fun," I say, putting my plate on the long table and taking a seat.

"Yeah," she agrees. "Kind of like this food. How's your project? Any progress towards growing us some chocolate or something?"

"It's not that fast," I say, looking at my plate.

She's right. We're living on rations that survived the wreck of the ship, which isn't much. We didn't need long-term food supplies as we grew everything we needed. Our ship was a generational colony ship designed for six generations to live and die on before reaching our ultimate destination. We were the third when the pirates attacked and caused us to crash here.

"Well this food sucks. You're our only hope Jolie-wan," Inga says, imitating Princess Leia's voice and we all laugh.

"Yeah," I agree, taking a spoonful of processed, vitamin-enriched protein slop.

"Soylent Green is made of people," Mei says.

"Oh gross!" Inga says, looking horrified.

"What, you didn't watch the old sci-fi collection?" Mei asks innocently.

"What's cooking?" Lana walks in and asks.

Lana is brunette, curvy, and screams her sexuality in every move. The wear and tear of living on a hellhole of a planet has somehow made her even sexier, which shouldn't be possible. Her skintight pants are torn in what would appear to be strategic places and her low cut shirt has rips and tears that tease without revealing too much.

"Same crap as always," Amara grumbles.

"Joy," Lana replies, grabbing a plate for herself.

"I'm working on it," I insist.

"So who's taking the epis?" Mei asks in her soft voice.

Everyone stares at their plate instead of answering. The

room is so quiet the click of the spoon against Lana's plate as she dips her food is the only sound.

The epis. Take it and the heat and hell of Tajss becomes bearable. Don't take it and it remains a burning hell that slowly dehydrates your body no matter how much you drink. The only problem is, take it and you can never leave. Ever. You're stuck on this planet for the rest of your life.

That's the decision point each of us is facing. Do we hold out and hope for rescue? Do we accept the fate of being here and take the epis? No one can decide for anyone else and the survivors have been split on the decision.

"Let's change the subject," Amara says.

"I haven't," I say, and everyone looks at me.

"Why not?" Mei asks.

Pursing my lips, I debate what to say. I can't tell them the truth, at least not all of it.

"Well, I'm waiting," I say. "I don't think the heat is that bad myself. I want to make the most of it and I'm worried it might slow my ability to tan."

They laugh and I smile.

I'm surrounded by friends but inside I'm alone. I can't open up with the truth to any of them. I'm hoping for rescue. Hoping for a knight in shining armor to come and sweep me off my feet. Steal my heart. Fill the empty ache in both my soul and my body. All of my body.

"So you're not going to take it at all?" Mei asks.

"No, not yet, maybe later. It's too... permanent. I'm thinking a rescue ship will be along in a bit and then we'd be stuck here. Besides, the supply is so limited. I figure, let the others have it first. I can always try later."

"You know you won't survive here without it?" Lana says.

"I'm fine, for now," I say.

"Does Calista know?" Inga asks.

"No, and please don't tell her," I say. "She's got enough on her mind and I'm fine."

Like having an alien baby with one of the only eligible bachelors on the entire planet. The sharp stab of jealousy cramps in my gut. Ugh, I hate being happy and jealous at the same time.

"I have to talk to Rosalind again," Amara says.

"Why?" I ask.

"I've got to get her to agree to mount an expedition outside the city limits," she replies.

"Outside? Like it's not dangerous enough inside?" I ask.

"Yeah, well, if we want those generators working, it's going to have to happen," she says.

"I'd go," I say. "What's out there you need?"

"I'm tracing the power conduits and they all lead to something on the outside. I'm not sure how it works but I need to take a look at whatever is there. If I'm right, there will be a switch or lever. Activate that and it will open up the conduit that activates the solar panels."

"Seems sensible," I say.

"Yeah, well, try to get Rosalind to agree to it."

"What's her issue?" I ask.

"Too dangerous, doesn't want to risk the manpower."

"But without the dome we can't secure the city," Lana says.

"Exactly," Amara replies.

"Damn," Lana says.

"I'll push her. She'll see sense, eventually," Amara says.

The conversation turns to small talk as we finish our dinner.

"I'm heading for my bunk," I say, standing up and going to rinse my dish.

They wish me good night and I wander deeper into the building to the small room I've claimed as my own. A few blankets on the floor, a small solar powered torch light, and a bowl with water to wash in. Home isn't much. Floor to ceiling windows allow me to stare out across the city and watch as the sun slowly drops below the horizon casting long, red-black shadows across empty streets. The jagged tops of buildings stab up into the sky like rotting teeth. It's sad looking out at what once was a thriving world, knowing that despite its capacity for a million or more, it's now home to only a few hundred refugee humans.

Survivors. We're all survivors. Castaways from a generation ship that was the only home any of us ever knew. Can I be homesick for a space ship?

Something moves in the distance on top of one of the tall buildings. I'm on the fourth floor looking up so I'm not sure if I saw something or not, but I think I did. It's probably Ladon and Calista. That's the building they're living in, up above the lab she and I commandeered.

Calista is so lucky. Damn, there I go again being jealous. A baby! How can I not be jealous? I was the one who was interested in settling down, finding the right man and starting a life together. Calista was more interested in books and work with little attention or time for dating.

Jealous or no, my heart swells thinking about the way he looks at her. He adores her, and she loves him too. They're perfect for each other and that makes me happy. Lying down on my pallet and closing my eyes, I send out my hopes that maybe, somehow, the one for me is out there and coming. I want someone to love me like Ladon loves Calista.

3

JOLIE

*W*aking up sucks. I'm stiff, sore, and so thirsty. No matter how much I drink, I'm thirsty. Every muscle aches and I know it's not just because of sleeping on the floor. My head hurts constantly and I'm almost always nauseous. Everything hurts and all I want to do is roll over and go back to sleep.

I sit and get the small bag I keep next to my bed. I take out salt and potassium tablets then a packet of powdered electrolytes that I pour into a glass of water. I drink it then lie back down and wait for the worst of the aches and pains to pass. Fifteen minutes later, I climb to my feet and stretch. Everything still aches but now it's uncomfortable, not debilitating.

I touch my toes a few times to work out the last of the kinks, and then wash up in my small basin of water before heading down to the dining room for breakfast. Mei is the only one at the table still eating when I walk in. She smiles when she sees me and I wave then go to fix myself some food. I sit down across from her.

"Morning," Mei says.

"Morning," I reply. "Everyone gone already or not up?"

"Mostly gone," she says. "I think Lana is still in bed."

"What a surprise," I snort.

"You okay?" Mei asks.

"Yeah, why?"

She shakes her head and puts her attention back on her food.

"Nothing, just checking," she says.

"Uh-huh, what's up?"

"You look, tired I guess. Your eyes are a bit dull, you know, just exhausted."

I smile and do my best to exude energy. "Yeah, didn't sleep great," I lie.

I slept fine. I slept too fine actually. Almost ten hours and I didn't want to get up when I did. Another sign of deep dehydration setting in. I'd be fine if I took the epis. Everyone who's taken it is doing great. Their bodies adjust to the heat, and they have more energy. Hell, some of them are even stronger than before, or so they claim. I haven't had a chance to run any tests on that so I'm skeptical.

Take the epis and the pain goes away. The aches, the nausea, the pounding headaches all gone—but then you're addicted. Worse, I'd be stuck here forever. No hope of a future beyond this planet. I know all the men who survived the crash and not a one of them appeals to me. So what would I do? Wait for the next generation to be born? Hope that Calista has a boy, wait twenty years, then see if we're compatible?

That's just creepy and wrong on so many levels I can't even begin to comprehend. It's too much to contemplate. I just have to hope a rescue ship comes. It won't be from earth, that would be impossible, but there were lots of colony ships sent out at the same time as ours and some of them had similar trajectories. They might have heard our distress calls.

There are also outposts on the rim of explored space. Mining planets and such where other humans live. There is a chance someone could come and take me off of this planet. Slim though it might be, it's my only hope of having a man and family of my own.

"I get that, I miss my bunk so much!" Mei says.

"Yeah," I agree. "We should work on better sleeping arrangements."

"Put it on the list of things," Mei smiles. "I'm sure it's on Rosalind's list, just low down below all those pesky survival items."

"Yeah, you're right," I agree.

I finish eating and clean my dishes. As I'm putting them away, I notice the tremors in my hands. Damn it, my muscles are weakening under the constant assault of the heat. That's bad. Mei walks up behind me and I pull my hand back, hoping she won't notice I was just staring at it.

"I'll see you at dinner," Mei says.

"Great, have a good day! Get lots done!"

"You too." She smiles then leaves.

I lean against the counter and contemplate the day. I'm supposed to go to the lab and continue working to find ways to make our small stash of seeds grow in the soil of this barren wasteland. A project that is on the order of squeezing blood from a rock. Right on the edge of impossible. So I can beat my head against the giant wall of trying to create our future, which sucks, or I can do something fun and exciting. Also necessary. Don't forget that!

I smile as I think about it. If we can get the dome working, then the damnable heat should be reduced. I think, maybe, that the shield will not only keep out predators but give us the power to control the weather inside. Besides, the place would look almost exactly like Gallifrey! Well, a worn down, beat up, crappy version of Gallifrey, but still who could pass up a chance to turn their new home into a *Doctor Who* set?

Well that makes the decision easy doesn't it? I go back to my room and pack a bag. In the kitchen, I grab extra supplies of electrolyte powders as well as salt and potassium. I fill three water bottles and then take a big cutting knife in case I need to defend myself against whatever is out there, which is a lot, but whatever. Rosalind won't approve this project but I'm not telling her. I can look and throw a lever or turn a knob. I'm a biochemist, how hard could it be to look at some machine and turn it on?

I leave the barracks, careful to make sure I don't run into anyone. No point in having to answer questions if I can avoid it. Lucky for me everyone is off doing their duties. Survival. Yay for crash landing on this hellhole of an empty, devastated planet. In all the episodes of *Star Trek*, especially the original series, every planet had eligible women for Kirk to make out with. Where's the planet filled with hunky men who want human women to adore? That's the planet I want to crash on. Is it really too much to ask that I find love?

Apparently, the universe has other plans. Yay for me, I guess. Shaking my head, I head down the empty street. As I walk, the sand encroaches on the asphalt piling up against the buildings where wind has slowly pushed it into the city. Decades of encroachment. Nature slowly works to eliminate the blight of intelligent life. It's early in the morning and sweat is still pouring out of me. It's well over a hundred degrees already and the sun has barely crested the horizon. I'm realizing that this was a stupid idea and I should be in my lab. The toasty ninety degrees of the dim lab beats hell out of this.

Too late now. Decision made girl! Keep your eye on the prize. Domes! Gallifrey! Doctor Who for the win! Oh Doctor, now there's a fate for sure. I could totally be a companion. I'm short, plucky, and full of smart remarks and look here, I'm already running off and getting myself into trouble. Now if I could just hear that whirring sound of the TARDIS arriving and a handsome sexy Doctor, like number ten, steps out and says 'Come with me' then everything would be perfect. That sexy Scottish accent and that smile and his hair! I could just melt thinking about the way my name would sound in his voice.

Sighing, I stop to drink some water. I'm on the edge of the city looking out across the vast desert of the planet. The city is surrounded by sand dunes. Everything is shades of red but it's really beautiful to look at. The striations of color are stunning. Deeper reds lie in lines against a shade that is almost white then a line that is a shade of yellow. The sun is making the sand sparkle and shine like diamonds are laid into the dune. If it wasn't so godawful hot I could like it here.

But it is and my head hurts, my body aches, and I really, really want a nap. No, no naps. I sip some more water then put the cap on. Amara said the conduits ran out from the edge of the city to . . . something. Trying to remember what she said exactly isn't coming back to me easily. My head hurts too much to think of what she was saying. Hmm, well conduits. That means some kind of pipes or protective lines right? So that's what I'm looking for. I should have gotten more details from her last night but I didn't think of it then and now it's too late. If I go back in the city and ask questions, it will be obvious what I'm doing.

So onward! When I come back, I'll be legendary! The one who found the switch. They'll cheer my name, maybe put up a statue by the big fountain at the city center. That'll be nice. I pace along the edge of the city looking for anything that looks like a conduit or anything at all that leads out into the desert while I dream of the accolades today's adventure will garner.

The sun is above the dunes leading me to guess I've been at this for over an hour and still haven't found anything that looks like a conduit. I stop again and drink more water with more of the supplements. My hand trembles then my entire arm starts shaking as I lift the water to my mouth. Water spills out of the bottle as I raise it and I have to put it back down. Tears threaten to fall but I'm too dry for them. Damn it I just want to fix this!

Putting both hands on the bottle, I'm able to get it to my mouth and take a long, refreshing drink. The coolness fills my mouth giving me a momentary respite from the parched feeling that doesn't stay gone for long. The pounding in my head recedes. I turn in a slow circle, looking for anything that would indicate what I'm looking for. Something flashes in the distance so I raise my hands to my eyes, shielding them from the sun. There, something is there.

Excitement bubbles up and I run towards it. I make about five steps before my knee gives out and I fall to the ground. Luckily, the sand is soft, but it gets in my mouth. I work my way back to my feet, spitting it out. Blah!

"I hate this place!" I scream, raising my fists at the sun.

Okay, that's better. I brush sand off myself then walk towards the flash I saw. I'm running on hope that it really was something and not a trick of the eye. Something comes into view. It's mostly buried in the sand but there's a definitive blocky shape about a hundred yards outside the city proper. It's set at the base of one of the massive sand dunes and I hope that it's what I'm looking for. That's the first thing. Second, of course, is that I can actually do something to fix it, turn it on, or something useful.

About three inches of metal sticks up above the sand. I kneel down beside it and brush the sand away, uncovering the top portion of a box that is about four feet long and three feet wide. It's made of a shiny metal, the same as the exteriors of most of the buildings. This has to be what Amara was talking about. If not, well it's something and maybe useful to some other thing. There are markings on it that I take to be words though I can't read them.

Digging into my pack, I find a plastic plate that I use as a shovel to dig out around the box. The sand keeps pouring back in behind each scoop making it so that I'm working at half speed. Every full scoop out, half of it backfills, making the job much more back-breaking than it should be. It takes a couple of hours I would guess, but eventually I've dug down two feet on all sides of the box and find that there are tubes running into it from the city and out on the far side.

The box itself is plain metal with no switches or levers. I sit down and the urge to cry almost overtakes me and probably would if I had anything left in me to cry with. There are bolts on each corner around the top of the box. I brought a few tools along so I dig until find a wrench. I open it up to the widest setting and it just barely fits over the nut. I pull on it and it doesn't budge. I move around and pull down, putting all of my weight on it. The bolt screams and creaks then moves, barely but as it does, the wrench slips and I'm thrown off and onto my backside.

"Damn it!" I cry out in frustration.

Then I hear a low growl and sand shifts down into the hole I've dug. The hairs on the back of my neck and arms stands up. My stomach tightens into a hard knot and bile rises into my throat. Stupid. I'm so, so stupid. I don't want to turn around. If I don't look it won't be real, but I know. I know deep down in my bones what's behind me and just how much trouble I'm in.

Slowly, I reach to my side and grip the handle of the chopping knife I brought with me. A knife. Wonderful. Why didn't I get a better weapon? Because it would raise too many questions. Why do you need a weapon in the lab Jolie? Well

27

you know, some of these plants around here are pretty mean. Shit.

The sand shifts again then one growl is followed by two more. I shift my feet as subtly as I can, finding purchase and getting ready. Once I have my feet pushed into the sand until it feels solid, I leap forward, hoping to clear the box and put it between me and whatever is wanting to eat me. My shins bark against metal as I fly over, not quite clearing it and the growls become like the weird howl of a dog and hiss of a cat blended into one horrifying sound.

I drop behind the box clutching the knife to my chest and hope with all my might that maybe the things after me are stupid enough to think out of sight means out of mind. Then one of them lands on top of the box above me and I scream. I'm looking up into row after row of razor sharp teeth and it drools on me. Disgusting, nasty, smelly drool with breath that smells like rotten meat. It looks down at me and growls.

I'm so screwed I do the only thing I can. I thrust up with the knife, gripping it tight in both hands and drive it into the throat of the thing above me. It howls now in pain and scrabbles back. I hear its feet as it slides across the smooth metal of the box then falls on the far side. More growls and the sand is pouring into the hole from either side. I look left and right and see two more of them coming around the hole.

Guster. God damn, nasty, killer guster. I'm an idiot. I shouldn't have come out here. Pressing myself back against the box, I rise to my feet then climb backwards onto it as they slowly close in. At least they're being cautious since I wounded the other one, but my only weapon is still stuck in it. Cause yeah, I'm just that smooth. What better way to prove that I shouldn't be out here?

The two guster feint in and back out. I try to come up with a plan. Any plan. Something that gets me the hell out of this situation. I can't outrun them. I can't out fight them. I can't do anything except scream. Scream and what? Hope someone will come to my rescue? Cause that's worked out so well since the ship crashed. Brilliant Jolie. You're smart, come up with a plan damn it!

Dominance. It's all about dominance and fear. Okay. I can do this. Taking a deep breath, I force myself to be calm. My heart rate is through the roof but I focus on calm. No fear. When the next one feints, I'll react then. Wait for it. Wait for it.

"HAH!" I scream, throwing my hands forward in what I hope is a threatening manner as the guster feints in.

I'm rewarded by it drawing back. My plan is working! I watch the other one out of the corner of my eye and repeat the action when it lunges. I get the same reaction but then they start circling. Shit, these things are too smart. They're moving out of time with each other until one of them is at my back and I can't keep them both in sight. The one in front moves in and I scream once more but, as I do, a cold realization hits me that the one behind me is coming in at the same time.

I duck and scream, this time in fear. Pain explodes as it impacts with me and I'm airborne flying towards the dune. Sorry Calista, I really do love you. Your baby will be as beautiful as you. Darkness encroaches on my vision and I'm fading. Probably for the best as I'm sure this next part is going to hurt. Just before I make contact with the ground, I see a Zmaj running. Oh my god, is Ladon coming?

Dazzling sunlight flashes on the edge of his blade as he glides in and attacks the guster. His wingspan seems bigger and is he a different color? Is that Ladon? Why doesn't he look the same? Good questions that all fade away as I crash and the impact jars my body. My head slams back and the last thing I see is a strange Zmaj standing over me.

4

SVERRE

*M*y patience is rewarded at last when a figure comes to the edge of the city. It has been many weeks that I've camped just outside the other Zmaj's territory and watched, waiting.

I move a bit under my camouflage upon spotting it and am amazed—it's her! My body stirs, desire and need awaken at the sight of her, making my thoughts a muddled mess.

Is this a trap? Did the warrior send her to draw me out? Even though I want to leap up and run to her, I'd best be cautious. I'll follow her. It seems unbelievable that she would be out here alone, so he could be watching, waiting to spring a trap on me. She wanders along the edge of the city and I follow, carefully maintaining my camouflage by moving along the sand. It's slow and I fall behind but I am able to keep her in sight.

She stops often and drinks. Her pauses allow me to keep her close, almost too close, making me worry again that it might be a trap. It doesn't matter. If it is, once I know for sure, I'll figure out a way to deal with it. Right now, I just need to know. She starts running towards something then falls on her face. I start to rise before I can stop myself, wanting to run to her side and protect her. I can't, not yet. It still might be a trap.

She climbs back to her feet and dusts herself off. My muscles relax when I see that she is okay. She continues on her way but moving slower now. Is she hurt? Anger pulses with each beat of my hearts at the thought. If she's hurt, I should go to her and help her. She needs me. But still it might be a trap. She's too close to the city. Prudence wins and I continue to follow. She stops, kneels, rummages in her pack and pulls out a round object, using it to start digging into the sand. She works diligently, hard, and I'm impressed at her dedication. It's fascinating watching her work.

Her fair skin has no scales, which is odd, but I've seen aliens without scales before, even if I only dimly remember them. She's small, compact but strong. She moves the sand and clears off an ancient box. It says something about being a relay but I'm not close enough to read it clearly. I'm absorbed in watching her, which is stupid. There is no forgiveness on Tajss, as I above all should know. I don't even see the guster until it's too late.

They surround her. She becomes aware of them a moment after I do and then she leaps to the far side of the relay box. One of them leaps on top of it, intent on feeding, but she lashes out and it leaps back, howling in pain with a gurgling sound. A piece of metal sticks out of its throat and the guster falls to the ground. The other two move more cautiously. They feint in and out, as she climbs on top of the relay and holds them off with pure bravado. I leap from the sand and run towards her but I'm too late.

They separate, making it impossible for her to keep them both in sight. The one behind her leaps and hits her in the back, sending her flying. I pull my lochaber. If this is a trap, then let my enemy spring it on me now. I will not stand by and watch her be killed. I take the one that hit her first, slicing through its rear legs in a single motion. I don't have time to finish it; the other is closing in on her. I leap into the air, spreading my wings to glide over the top of the box. I whirl my lochaber as I come down and hold it two handed, driving it into the base of the second guster's neck. She whispers something that sounds like "Ladon" as I land.

I jerk my lochaber free then whirl towards the first one. It's crawling away so I finish it before I go to her side. She lies in an unmoving heap against the sand dune. Her eyes are closed and I'm not sure if she's breathing. Leaning in close, I place my ear next to her mouth and hear the soft hiss of air moving in and out. I look around, waiting for the trap, but if it's to be sprung, they're too late. No one comes.

Could I have been wrong?

Moments pass and nothing happens. At last, I turn back and kneel beside her. The dark fur on her head is splayed around her like a halo. She is beautiful and peaceful lying here in the shade of the dune. What am I going to do? I have to help her but how do I do that? Home. I'll take her home. She's mine. I start to scoop her up but stop.

No. I don't deserve her. My punishment for my failures is to be alone. To suffer in my solitude and see what becomes of my brethren because of my mistakes. My dishonor haunts me from the fog of my memories.

This is now. Live in now, not then.

Hissing, I gather her into my arms and pull her close to my chest. She's burning hot. Unbelievably hot, but I'm too close to the city to take time and decide if this is her native state. It doesn't feel unpleasant. I like the way she folds against me and there are soft mounds on her chest that stir desires long dormant.

Shifting her weight to best advantage, I run, spreading my wings and covering my tracks with my tail as I go. The distance to home is great and carrying her weight will slow me down, but I don't want to stay this close to another's city. The more distance between us and it, the better.

I run until exhaustion sets in. The sun is low in the sky by the time distance between us and the city is great enough that I feel safe to make camp. Laying her down on the sand, I debate how to shelter her. She won't be able to bury herself in the sand like I would and I don't know the terrain. If I could find an oasis, that would be best, probably. There would be wood and things I could build with but I don't see anything like that in sight.

When I touch her skin, she is still burning hot and moans softly. Leaning close, her breath is shallow. I rest my head on her chest and it takes me a few tries before I can find the sound of a heart. I only hear one, another oddity. Her skin is soft. Too soft, strange and alien in its exposed, unprotected nature. Trailing my fingers across it, my prime penis stiffens. It's so enticing, I want to explore every bit of her but I can't let myself become distracted no matter the urges and desires that rage.

She's too hot. I'm certain of it and I think this is part of the reason she has not regained consciousness. I want to hear her voice again. That beautiful musical sound still echoes in my mind and I need it. Her arms and her face are burning and I need to cool her. My body is built to exchange heat so if I can get our skin in contact it should pull the heat from her and allow her own system to cool itself once it's not overloaded.

I have no other options. It has to work. First, I need to get her out of the restrictive clothing she wears. The cloth covering her chest has shiny fasteners that run down the middle. Pulling on them, they don't give but as I do, I notice

33

that the cloth opens up slightly like there is a tiny hole. I lean in close, study what I'm seeing, and realize that the shiny piece slides through a gap in the fabric. It takes a few attempts to figure it out but I glean that it's actually quite simple. The shiny piece is turned to the side then it slides through the hole. Once I've managed the first one the others follow quickly.

Her skin under the cloth has a nice golden hue to it instead of the angry red of her exposed skin. This confirms my belief she is too hot and needs to be cooled. The exposed skin is trying to exchange heat with the air but failing. Below her neck are two mounds of flesh that are covered by more cloth that is white. Hooking my fingers under it, I pull up but it stretches and then slips off my fingers, slapping against her flesh.

Strange. I don't know what kind of material this is. It's soft yet stretchy. I grab it again and pull, keeping a firmer grip this time. The mounds of flesh fall up as they are freed from the restraints of the cloth but it reaches a limit and won't go any further. There are bands that wrap around behind her. I don't see any fasteners or way for it to connect on the front even after I carefully inspect it. Gently I put it back into place. I will deal with it in a bit.

The pants she wears are tight fitting and hug her waist. There is another shiny round piece at the front below her stomach. It's easy to see that it works the same as the cloth that covered her chest and I unfasten it without trouble. When I pull down to separate the fastener, a piece of metal comes into view. It looks like teeth that interlock with each other and as I pull down on the sides, they release their grip one to another and an odd metallic sound emerges. This loosens her pants enough that I'm able to grab them and pull them down off her legs.

A musky scent fills the air and I'm extremely aroused. Her legs are smooth without a scale in sight. My thumbs drag along the soft skin of them as I remove her pants and my cock becomes so tight I almost burst. I have to look away and focus on the danger we're both in to calm myself. Her pants hang up on the protective wear she has on her feet so I turn my attention to them.

They're made from the hide of some animal but not one I've ever seen. Brown and dull in color with an odd texture. A thick string crisscrosses down the top section, which rises up onto her ankles. The bottoms are a harder material with ridges cut into it. Helpful looking for getting traction but probably not of much use in the sand. Tracing the strings, they meet at the top and are tied into a knot. Finding this, it doesn't take long for me to loosen them and slide them off of her feet.

Her pants come off easily once the protective gear is out of the way and she is mostly nude. Heat flows and exchanges best at the extremities and there are still small pieces of cloth on her feet so those are next to be removed. Her feet are shocking once they're fully revealed. They're dainty, small, and have no scales. They end in five individual toes instead of three like my own and there are no claws. Thin membranes of what might once have been bone claws cover the tops of the tips but they are short, not sharp, and a bright red color that contrasts sharply with the dull red of the sand. I raise one up close to my eyes and inspect it. Strange and oddly enticing.

She moans and shifts so I put her foot back down and return to my task at hand. Letting myself be distracted by interest and desire is not acceptable. I'm stronger than that and must remain focused on what matters. Save her life first. The stretchy cloth still covers her chest and another small bit is around her middle but, for my purposes, she is fine. Lying down next to her, I pull her body close to mine, placing an arm and a leg over the top of her and angling myself so I rest mostly over her body.

My body exchanges heat well. I'm built for the temperatures here and she is not. Pressing against her, my body absorbs her heat, sucking it out of her and then filtering it through my own system. Her skin is soft. Too soft, too enticing, my thoughts cloud with desire resting against her. It's been too long since... no, I will not go back there. Some memories the bijass can keep. I don't want to recall them.

My head rests on top of hers. The scent of it fills my nostrils and involuntarily my cock grows erect again. My erection presses against her leg and the urge to consummate with her is almost overwhelming. Gritting my teeth, I resist the desires but my hands drift along her soft skin. My fingertips tingle as they pass along her leg, up across her hips and stop at the unprotected mounds on her chest. She makes a muffled sound and moves closer to me.

Stop.

I force myself to quit touching her, quit moving, and focus my thoughts on my purpose. She is beautiful and highly erotic, arousing me in ways that I can barely contain but I'm not a monster. I will not force myself on her, especially not while she's unconscious. Besides, I don't deserve to have her in that way. I'm saving her, that's it. Feelings more than thoughts, concepts with no tie to specific moments, push through the fog of the bijass and remind me that I'm not worthy. I've done terrible things.

Her temperature is dropping and as it does her breathing eases. She rolls to her side, pressing close against me and I feel sure that she's now simply sleeping. Her body is recovering. I've saved her. Good, perhaps this is a start on my path to redemption. Her backside with its soft, so soft luscious mounds presses hard against my groin. My erect cock presses in between the soft globes and if I was to slide it past the clothes I wear, I would enter her. I won't, no matter how much I want to.

I lay awake protecting her through the night. In the morning, we'll continue the journey home.

5

JOLIE

*M*y head isn't hurting as much as usual. That's nice, so much better than when I normally wake up. I lie still enjoying the freedom from pain before opening my eyes. The bed is unusually comfortable as well. Maybe I'll sleep a while longer. I turn to pull the blanket up then stop. Something is weird. The blanket is too... furry? I crack one eye open to figure that out, still hoping to go back to sleep.

Is it still night? The light is dim, like its late evening or early in the morning. My room is only this dark during those times. The blanket over me isn't mine. What the hell is this? Fear freezes me in place for an instant gripping my stomach in a tight knot and sending chills racing through my limbs. Opening both eyes, I look around without moving.

A furry blanket is on top of me and I'm lying on more furs. The wall next to me looks like it's made of stone, not the smooth metal and glass of my room. I'm lying on my side facing a stone wall that is illuminated with a soft orange glow from somewhere behind me. My heart pounds like a jackhammer in my chest and it's all I can do to keep myself from hyperventilating. Dim memories of being carried and bouncing emerge from the clutches of my mind. Wasn't that a dream? Am I dreaming now? That has to be it. One of those lucid dreams where you know you're dreaming and it all seems too real, right?

I make a very slow roll over to my back listening for any sound of disturbance at my movement. Now I'm staring at a ceiling that is maybe four feet over me. It's also plain rock with shadows dancing from the illumination source. Nothing happens, no sounds to clue me in and no idea how I got here. Rolling on to my side, I'm face to face with a thin curtain. I can see a room on the other side of it, a room filled with shapes made vague by the drapery.

What do I do now? Okay, Jolie what options do you have? One, lie here and wait. Wait for what? No clue. Okay that's not a great idea. Option two; I climb out of here ready to face anything and everything. Well, that at least has the attraction of being in motion. Lying here waiting just doesn't work for me and if whatever or whoever brought me here wanted to hurt me it isn't going to do any good to lie here until it happens.

Moving my body aches and I remember the guster. One of them hit me and I was flying then a Zmaj showed up except it wasn't Ladon! The memory of the Zmaj hits like a thunder stroke. A different Zmaj! Well, good, right? Ladon is cool, so this guy is probably a nice guy too, right? I mean he saved me and that is pretty much a re-creation of how Calista and Ladon met. So? So far so good.

Feelings of relief relax the knots of fear and tension in my stomach and muscles. As the fear passes, a low level of desire floods in behind it. Great, I'm horny. Just what I need as a distraction. Okay, push that aside, because right now I need to meet this new Zmaj and figure out where the hell we are. And my friends will be worried. I need to get back to the city and let them know I'm okay. Looking back on it, leaving without telling anyone what I was doing ranks in the top ten dumbest things I've ever done. If I had told someone though, they would have stopped me, so that's a catch twenty-two if there ever was one.

Oh well. I'm here and hey, I'm about to meet a new alien. So take the win and let's roll with it. Swinging my legs off the edge of the makeshift bed, my bruised muscles cry out in discomfort and a groan escapes my lips. Something scrapes outside the curtain as I drop my legs underneath the edge of it. I'm reaching for the curtain to pull it aside when it's jerked open. I'm inches away from my rescuer and I yelp.

I don't mean to. It slips out mostly because I'm startled and he's so big and so in my space without warning. His eyes widen and he hisses in response. Tilting his head to one side, he leans down so that we're eye to eye. His eyes are fascinating, almost a turquoise color that is gorgeous and deep like a rich, sweet pool of water. His scales are different from Ladon's, having a blue hue to them and the edges are a bright, rich, almost fluorescent green. The wings on his back rustle with a soft leathery sound.

"Hi!" I exclaim, raising a hand in greeting.

He says something. Of course, I don't speak Zmaj so I have no clue what it is. I'm going to assume he's saying something like 'hi' back to me. It could be 'I want to eat you for dinner' but who wants to start a first meeting out on that note? We stare at each other for what starts to feel like forever. I'm waiting for him to move or say something and maybe he's waiting for the same. Either way, I decide to take the bull by the horns.

"So," I say. "What's a sexy alien man like you doing in a place like this?"

I smile my best and most friendly smile and push myself forward. My feet barely touch the ground when I'm completely on the edge of the bed. He moves back enough that I'm able to slide the rest of the way out and stand. He towers over me but I'm used to that. Almost everyone is taller than me.

The room looks like a converted cave that has been outfitted with at least the rudiments of comfort. Shelves line the stone walls filled with objects and a handful of what look like books. The floor is covered with dark brown furs that I recognize as coming from the bivo herds. On some of the cabinets are small bowls with a floating flame in them that is the source of illumination. A table and two chairs are to the left and behind the Zmaj. Several metal objects lie on it as well as some cloths and uh, goop?

I push past the Zmaj and walk over to one of the shelves. I pick up what looks like a tiny skull and look it over. The thing still has nasty looking fangs and looks like it might have come from a snake. The next piece I grab is metal, cylindrical in shape, with a diamond shaped end on one side and the other is a flat bottom. Turning it over in my hands, I examine it but can't figure out any rhyme or reason to what it might be or do.

"This looks nifty, what is it?" I ask over my shoulder.

He watches me still standing where I left him. Smiling I wave the stick thing in his direction but he doesn't respond.

"Not the talkative type?" I ask. "That's okay; I'll talk for both of us."

He's big and imposing. Also, there's something about him that excites the low level of desire I woke up with causing it to pull at my attention. To push thoughts like that aside I put all my attention on the objects in front of me. Suddenly it hits me and I look down at myself and realize I'm not wearing my clothes. The clothes I have on are loose, flowing, and definitely not what I was wearing when the guster attacked. Looking from them to him my skin burns hot knowing that he had to change them and that means he's seen me naked. Embarrassment burns while jealousy stabs in behind it because I'd really like to see his massive, well-muscled and colorful body too. Only fair right?

"Uh, clothes?" I ask holding up a piece of the flowing cloth and pointing at it.

He shrugs then nods his head. Okay then. This language barrier sucks.

"Well yeah, uh, thanks?" I say.

We stare at each other and I debate whether anything got across to him or if he's just filling in blanks. Maybe he's just thinking I'm nuts. Or wondering what I am. I've seen his race before because I know Ladon but he's probably never seen a human before. Well crud, I hadn't thought about that.

"I'm Jolie," I say pointing at myself then I point at him. "You?"

He watches my motions, his head moving along with each one and he looks like he's studying me. I guess. I really didn't ever pay much attention to Ladon's mannerisms so I can't claim to be an expert. He hisses, a soft sound like air escaping from a balloon and then I realize he's talking. He speaks softer than Ladon does, very quiet, so I step closer to make sure I hear him.

There's a scent to him when I get closer. It's not musk, that's a human scent, this is something exotic, enticing, pulling at my senses. Smelling it makes my lizard brain jump into hyper drive. Hmm, bad choice of phrasing. Okay, it makes my primal urges much more prominent. It's almost like a spice, or really good food that you've never tasted but can't wait to savor. The odor pulls me in and I want to inhale more of it. I'm two paces away from him and close my eyes inhaling deeply through my nose, letting the scent fill me. He hisses and this time I can tell it's almost my name, if I was to drag out the J into a really long consonant sound and leave off the O. It sounds like Jjjjjjlie. Opening my eyes, I smile broadly and nod excited.

"Yes! J-O-lie," I say emphasizing the O sound for him.

He frowns, his thinly scaled lips purse and his eyes narrow giving him a definitive look of concentration. It's exciting watching him move his mouth to form the vowels.

"Jjjjj-oooo-leee," he says.

I jump up and down clapping my hands.

"Perfect!" I exclaim.

He smiles or at least partially smiles. It's not a full smile, I've seen Ladon smile most any time he's looking at Calista and it's not that so let's call it a grin. He grins. Yeah, I can go with that.

"Jjjjooooleee," he says again, smoothing out the sound of my name.

I clap and grin encouraging his efforts. "Jolie," I repeat after him, pointing to myself.

He touches my chest between my breasts. My breath catches and my heart stops at his touch. All my attention goes to that mostly innocent point of contact between us. I don't drop my eyes, I don't dare to, desire is threatening to roar into a raging fire that I know will consume me and I'll do something stupid.

"Jjjooolee," he says, tapping his finger lightly against me.

I nod and swallow hard trying to force moisture back into my mouth and throat, which feels as dry as it ever has. The two of us stare into each other's eyes and, for a moment, it's like I'm falling into those beautiful pools. The urge to kiss him is strong and almost I give in but just as I'm about to he pulls his hand away and steps back. A hiss is followed by words that sound harsh and the moment is over.

He turns away from me and I don't understand it but it looks and feels like he storms to the small table where he sits down. Grabbing up the objects on the table he cleans them while pointedly ignoring me. Upset comes and goes. If I knew what was going on, I might be upset but as far as I can tell he's just a grump so why let that bother me? Shrugging I decide to continue my investigation of his home instead of worrying about it.

"No problem!" I say but he ignores me. "Going to entertain myself over here."

His focus is on inspecting the metal piece in his hands so I look for something else interesting. There are dozens of things on the shelves. Scrolls that look like they're made of hide which are covered with drawings that I don't really understand but look like they could be specs for a machine. A few actual books but these are so worn I'm afraid to open them. I touch the pages of one and they start to crumble so I set those aside. I'm not looking to be destructive, just to get a feel for who I'm with.

Hidden behind a pile of bones I spy a carved wooden box. It's covered with crude shapes and symbols none of which means anything to me. Why would they? This isn't my home and I have no idea really of the culture that existed here in the past. When I touch the box, a thrilling tingle runs up my arm. The Zmaj is behind me cleaning and apparently paying no attention as I paw through his things but the way this was hidden makes it feel special. Like something that was buried and hidden for a reason and I feel naughty picking it up. Looking it over, I see a fastener and what looks like a lid so I set it down on the cabinet. I push the fastener, which takes me a moment to figure out how it works. It pushes to one side and then I'm able to lift the lid.

Inside the box is a material that looks and feels like velvet. I don't think it is that, but that's what it reminds me of. Lying in the center of it is a shiny metal badge. It's bright and multicolored. The flickering flame makes rainbows dance across the shield. Oh my god, it's a shield! It's like Star Trek, the communicators they wore on their uniforms, not shaped the same but it has a swooping shape that's kind of like it. Or Nike! Yeah, the swoop is made of a reflective metal that spins with multiple colors as the light hits it. Taking it out of the box, it's surprisingly heavy for its small size. It must weigh close to a pound while only being two, to two and a half inches long and about an inch and a half wide.

I flip it over to see how it fastens and find the back is smooth too. Hmm, lifting it up I turn it back and forth watching the light play across it. It's fascinating the way the light breaks down when it hits it. Almost like it's covered with an oil-like substance that reflects into different colors. The chair behind me hits the wall and then I'm in his grip and being spun around. Words flow from his mouth, harsh sounding, gruff, all of them with elongated s sounds.

Adrenaline pumps into my body. My heart beats in double time and my muscles shake with the need to flee. He's shaking his head as he speaks. Gripping my wrists together roughly in one hand, he pulls my arms up over my head forcing me up onto my tiptoes. He takes the badge from me and waves it in front of my face still speaking rapidly.

"I don't understand," I say as tears well in my eyes.

I do my best to choke them back. He pulls me closer forcing me to move towards him on my tiptoes. He shakes me, not violently, but enough that it's scary. He speaks more but the language barrier stops any understanding.

"I'm sorry," I say as I feel the first tear fall down my cheek.

He stops talking, and it looks like he's staring at the tear. My heart pounds as I'm gasping air and I wait for whatever comes next. I'm completely under his control and that fact really hits me for the first time. I don't know where we are, how to get back to my friends, or have any ability to survive out here that doesn't depend on him. Something changes in his face. I can't really put my finger on any one thing but it goes from angry to something that looks like regret. He steps back one step putting a small amount of space between us then he lowers his arm until I'm back on the flats of my feet. Only then does he let go of my wrists.

He says something, his voice is soft, and he doesn't meet my eyes. He holds the badge up, waves it, then shakes his head staring down the entire time. He shrugs then steps past me and picks up the box that the badge came out of. As I watch, he carefully places the badge back into the box, closes it, then rests his hand on it while bowing his head.

Is it sacred? Like some kind of religious artifact? If he wasn't so alien and dragon like I'd think he was praying. Do alien dragons pray? He picks the box up and there is a definite air of reverence. He turns towards me, speaks still without looking up, then shakes his head. He holds the box up between us, says the same thing again shaking his head side to side this time to emphasize his point, then walks over to the table. He sits down then puts the box next to the wall on the far side of him.

"Well, all right then," I say taking a deep breath. "That was interesting."

He doesn't say anything, but he does glance at me quickly.

"Anything else I'm not supposed to touch?" I ask.

He picks up a tube and then his cloth, which he dips in the paste and starts polishing. My belly rumbles loudly, and he stops mid-motion.

"Yeah, uhm, food?" I ask miming eating something when he glances in my direction.

He says something, and it sounds like a question. There's a lilt at the end of it, anyway.

"Food?" I ask miming again. "You know, give me something good to eat?"

I smile hoping to relieve any remaining tension over whatever the hell just happened. He repeats the same question. Well it sounds the same to me so I'm assuming it is. I pat my belly, mime food, then ask him again. Slowly he sounds out the word.

"Fffooooddd," he says.

I nod enthusiastically. "Yes!"

He pats his belly then mimes eating in the same way I had a moment ago and I encourage him with more enthusiastic nodding. He seems to get my intent as he stands up and walks over to a chest I haven't explored yet. Though thinking of the last box I opened maybe I should avoid anything that is closed. He opens the chest and my stomach grumbles anew as the scent of edible things fills the space.

He pulls out a leather wrapped package and opens it to reveal small, leathery looking strips. He picks up one and tosses it into his mouth chewing while motioning the package towards me and nodding his head. I take one and put it in my mouth. Spice overwhelms my taste buds. The meat really is like leather, I chew on it trying to break it down so I can eat it but tears flow freely as the spice burns its way into my mind and my teeth are apparently ineffective. I can't break it down.

Exhaustion swells up and I'm too tired to think anymore. I spit out the meat into my hand and shake my head side to side wiping my tears on the sleeve of my shirt. My belly grumbles loudly but this isn't food no matter how badly I need to eat. Or drink, anything to drink would be welcome at this point. Shaking my head, I look at him then turn away unable to meet his eyes.

Walking to the back of the room I climb into the bed and pull the curtain closed. This sucks. This sucks so much. Maybe if I sleep a bit, it'll seem better. I drift off to the sound of my grumbling belly. Sleep is my only escape.

6

SVERRE

*S*he climbs back into my bed and closes the curtain while moisture leaks from her eyes. An ache forms in my chest watching her. She needs to eat. She needs epis. I carefully wrap the dried bivo meat and return it to the chest.

My planet is killing her. I can't deny what I see. I don't know her race but the signs are clear for anyone who cares to look. Her skin is lax and too red. Her internal temperature is burning and it's very apparent she's not made for this environment. The only answer for her is epis and I have none. My body is adapted to the heat and I don't need it often. Harvesting it alone is almost impossible and who do I have to help me? No one.

A possessive desire boils inside my gut that I have no other outlet for besides anger. Undirected, irrational, it eats at me filling me with a need to destroy something. I concentrate and focus on breathing. A facet of the bijass. I know that's all it is, but it doesn't make the feelings, the desires, any less real. I am still surprised after all these years by the bijass' power to consume me. I shouldn't have gotten rough with her. That was a mistake. She doesn't deserve to be treated like that and yet when I saw the badge in her hand I lost control.

I haven't looked at or touched that badge in decades. It's been hidden away—that's how I like it. A relic of the past that belongs there. Memories stir when I see it and I don't want to remember. Who I was then is not who I am now. I'm not that person any longer. That person did terrible things. That person is guilty of crimes that I can't and won't face. I don't have to because I'm no longer him. Those mistakes are still being paid for. Every time I walk out the door and see my planet empty. Every day that I wake up alone and know that my race is slowly dying, I pay the price. I don't remember the details. It's enough to know that it was all my fault.

The lights outline her shape behind the curtain. The rise of her hip, the fall along her side, the rise back to her shoulder outlined in silhouette is beautiful. As I push past the anger pulsing through me, desire replaces it. She is mine. I must have her. I knew it when I saw her. I know in part this is the bijass, the primal instinct to collect and hoard things that please me but my feelings are more than that. If that's all it was, I would take her and she would be mine. But I am not an animal. I am a man.

I want to win her over. I must treat her with kindness and show her that I'm not a monster. I wonder how much the other Zmaj has revealed to her. How much of our culture, of what we once were, does she know? She doesn't seem to know our language or, if she does, she's doing an amazing job of playing dumb. I don't think she's doing that. I watch her eyes and there's not a hint of understanding when I speak to her.

Her language is musical and has so many soft sounds in it. It feels strange in my mouth when I try to say them. Her name is like that of a delicate flower and rolls off my tongue. I sound it out again speaking very softly so as not to risk waking her up. Saying it makes me smile. Feeling more myself, I rise up and look around my home.

This is what I'm reduced to. Once I was a leader. Once my home was one of the finest on the planet and I had multiple workers who cared for my every need. Now there is only me, alone, tucked away in this cave with the few amenities I've allowed myself. This is not sufficient for her. I can do better than this. Moving as silently as I can, I stand outside the curtain to the bed and listen to her breathing. It's smooth and even, so I believe she is deeply asleep.

I will use this time to improve the space. That will show her I am not a monster. I'm sure she must have been terrified when I lost control. If I want her to accept me, to choose me as I've chosen her, sssshe must see more of who I really am. Not the monster that I can be when in the grip of the bijass. As a plan comes to me, a smile forms with it. I will surprise her.

THE ROCK SLIDES BACK INTO PLACE BLOCKING THE ENTRANCE to my cave. I walk down the tunnel then slide through the curtain into the room I call home. Moving quietly and hoping that Jolie is still asleep, I stop once I'm through and check the still-closed curtain to the bed. Her silhouette still rests there, apparently not having moved at all. Perfect.

I set down the pack I'm carrying and take out the flowers I've spent the past two days gathering. I place them around the room, adjusting them until I'm finally satisfied. The normally plain and dingy place is now an explosion of color that carefully blends from one hue to the next as the eye travels. It's perfect. I want her to see that though my home is harsh and can be quite deadly, it is also a place of beauty. Beauty almost as pure as hers.

I close my eyes and inhale deeply of the flowers' perfume. Pleasant memories stir beneath the fog of the bijass but nothing rises to the surface. I let it go. Memories are for yesterday. The room looks more welcoming, and I feel certain she will appreciate it when she wakes. Now for the next part of my plan. I don't have epis for her to take but I do have a small store of guster meat. Guster lay their eggs in the same caverns where epis grows and feed on the sismis that live in them. The meat of a guster is infused with epis and will at least help her feel better. It's not the same as taking the epis directly but it can assist her metabolism in dealing with the heat.

Some of my collection covers the fire pit. I don't use it often. I smoke a lot of meat after I kill it and don't have to worry about it for weeks. When I've cleaned the pit, I breathe out, releasing flame from the glands deep in my throat. While the fire crackles, I dig through my storage chest and find the guster meat. I have it wrapped in oiled cloth to keep it from spoiling but still check it when I find it to make sure it hasn't started to turn.

It smells fine which is good because I don't know what I would do to keep her safe if I had to go out hunting. Next, I dig out a small, flat piece of metal to cook it on. I retrieve a pouch of herbs and then I'm ready. The metal heats and, while it's doing so, I season the meat, then lay it on the sizzling hot surface. The odor of spice and meat fills the room competing with the fragrance of the flowers. A smile spreads across my face as I hear her stir behind the curtain.

I sear the meat on each side, turning it frequently until it cooks through. This won't fix Jolie but it will help, buying time while I figure out a solution. She needs epis and I'll have to get some for her, somehow. I'll handle that problem later. Now I need to make it right with her for the way I treated her. She doesn't deserve my aggression. I was wrong and I need her to know that I realize it.

I pull the meat from the pan as the curtain slides aside. She swings her legs out of the bunk, and I watch as she looks around. Her eyes widen as her mouth spreads into a big smile. She turns her head from side to side, taking in all the flowers and decorations I gathered for her pleasure. She speaks rapidly and I don't understand the words, but the sound of her voice creates a swelling sensation in my chest. I smile and she nods, sliding out of the bed to her feet. She comes close to me then reaches out and places a hand on my chest.

The world stops when she touches me. Everything is frozen into this moment. The heat of her skin warms me through the cloth of my shirt. A tingle emanates from where her fingertips rest against me and my cock stiffens in slow motion, moving at the same speed as time. My hearts beat once. I don't want this moment to end. She's touching me of her own free will. The rich, creamy brown pools of her eyes look deep into my own and I want to kiss her.

I stop myself as I lean in with every intention of our lips meeting. She has not invited me in. A touch is not an invitation to more. Fear of rejection but more, of pushing her too far, kills the joy and sensations of her touch. I've already made mistakes with her—I won't make more. She must see me as the man I am. She is a treasure to be loved, respected, and cared for, not something to be taken lightly.

I want, more than anything right now, to hear my name on her lips. Hearing her say my name in her musical voice, the way it will roll off her tongue. . . the anticipation fills me with a lightness.

"Sverre," I say tapping my chest. I repeat this three times saying my name slowly.

She watches, studying my lips, so I repeat my name trying to break it down into the components sounds.

"Serrrrre," she tries, but it's not right.

Smiling in what I hope is an encouraging way I repeat myself several more times and she mimics along.

"Sverre," she says, her mouth carefully forming my name while her fingers still rest lightly on my chest.

"Jj-ooo-lee," I say, struggling to form the soft sounds correctly.

Her smile is all the reward I could ask for. Her face transforms into something exquisite, delicate, bright, consuming all my thoughts and attention. Her blunt teeth shine bright and white, her full lips spread, my cock throbs with need and the urge to kiss her fills me once more but I resist.

I motion to the table. She nods but her fingers linger on my chest. Does she want me to kiss her? Does she want more? I wish I could understand her language. Dim memories stir and I know with certainty that before the devastation I could have understood her. Before, when we had technology, when the old things still worked, language was no barrier. Now it's a gulf separating us, limiting our communication to primitive gestures and desperate attempts to be understood. Anger flares deep in my guts at the impotence of it, and that vague sense of what I've lost. Watching her move to the table, the way she walks, the way her hips sway give focus to better feelings. She bends over part way to pull the chair out and the round softness of her backside pushes aside all other thoughts. I recall how her body swells back there and the softness of how it feels. My cock throbs uncomfortably and I have to shake myself.

Food. Focus on the food. She sits while I concentrate on placing the meat on plates, then the plates on the table, one in front of each of us. She leans over hers and I hear her inhale deeply.

"Mmmm," she says.

It's a soft, sensual sound that does nothing to help me keep my mind on the food. My cock stirs and it is an act of will to focus on anything else. I place two cups from my shelf on the table, and then rummage in my storage trunk. I find the bag I want which is sewn together so that it has a small point, which is capped at the end to contain its contents. I pour some white liquid from the bag into the cups then hang it on the wall.

"Eat," I say motioning from the plate to her.

She looks down then up at me but doesn't start eating. I motion again and she shrugs, waiting for something, but I have no idea what. Frustration builds and the soft anger at our inability to communicate returns. I love the sound of her voice but can only imagine how wonderful it would be if the musicality of it was conveying concepts and ideas. I take up a piece of the meat off my own plate and place it in my mouth then chew it. After I do I motion for her to do the same this time more emphatically. She has to eat; the trace amounts of epis in the meat will make her feel better. I need her to eat it.

Sadness passes across her face, but she picks up a piece of the meat, even if her shoulders drop as she does and the smile fades away. The meat passes her lips. Full, sweet lips that I want nothing more than to explore the taste of. It's distressing watching her start to chew. Resignation is on her face as she does, and I can see she is bracing herself for something bad. I know with certainty she expects the meat to make her sick, but this will be different. It has to be, because I don't have any other options.

Epis was the lifeblood of our planet. The galaxy came to our door for it. It was also our downfall. I need it to be a savior again. It has to save her, turn around the harm that the harshness of my planet is doing to her body. She looks up and meets my eyes as she chews. It's working. I can see it in the way her face lights up, the glint in her eyes, the increase in the speed of her chewing. It's working, thank the stars. I nod encouraging her and point at the plate motioning that she should eat more.

She does. I eat with her but I don't need the epis so I eat slowly. She eats two pieces then starts talking, gesturing as she does. She nibbles at the next piece of meat without stopping the flow of her conversation. Feelings of peace and contentment fill my thoughts as she talks. I don't know what she's saying but I don't care. I can be happy just listening to her.

She reaches for the glass and takes a drink, which causes her to cough and splutter. Damn, I hadn't thought to try to warn her about the effects of the lissta. It burns when you swallow it but it has restorative properties. She pounds her chest, looks at me, says something, then laughs. Frowning at my own stupidity in not warning her I grab a cloth and wipe her mouth for her. She gives me an odd look that I don't know how to interpret. She says something.

"I wish I could understand you," I say. "I would love to know your thoughts."

I finish wiping her cheek then place the cloth next to her. She takes up the glass and this time she sips slowly and doesn't react as badly. She leans back in her chair and smiles. She points to the glass, makes the mmm sound, then rubs her belly. I smile and she nods enthusiastically. Words may be a barrier but we're finding ways to communicate. She eats the rest of her meat so I put the last two pieces from my plate onto hers.

She waves her hands and shakes her head side to side. She needs it so I motion at it then at her miming eating. Again, she does the hand wave and head shake. Hissing I point sharply. I know what's best here. There is only trace amounts of epis in the meat and she's not eaten enough for the effect to last more than a few hours. It has to be consumed in suffi-cient amounts to build up in her system.

She resists further. She is my treasure, and she is resisting me. Unexpected, primal rage roars to life as my desire to protect her is denied. Rising to my feet, I point at the meat then at her hissing loudly as I do. My wings rustle and my tail is shifting from side to side. I lean over the table, angry and intending to make her eat it. I know what's best for her. If she doesn't eat enough now there won't be enough in her system and there isn't enough left for a second meal.

She cowers, leaning back as she crouches down in her chair, raising her hands in a protective gesture. Primal fog fills my brain to see her cowering. The rise of her chest, its unprotected mounds moving up and down rapidly in time with her breath, the smell of her creates a war of emotions in me. A desire to dominate and own what is mine wars with the rational man. She is mine and must obey but she is her own and I must treasure and respect her.

She takes the meat and eats it at last but, as she does, a drop of moisture falls from her eye and rolls down her cheek. Watching it fall a sick feeling of nausea forms in my gut and the fog clears. I've frightened her. It's clear as day she's afraid. She chews the meat then slips out of the chair as I fall back into my own. She climbs into the bed without looking at me and slides the curtain closed.

Staring at it, I don't know how to fix what I've done. I didn't intend to frighten her or ever cause her harm. She is something to be treasured, valued, but never mistreated. I want what's best for her but how do I tell her that? Gestures, grunts, motions that don't communicate the complexity of ideas I need her to understand. How else could I explain to her about the epis? The healing properties of the meat or how she had to eat enough for the effects to last?

Am I a man or am I too far gone to the bijass? That's the

heart of the question. How lost to the fog am I? Can I break free of the regression? Can any of us?

Somehow, I know she's the key. She awakens thoughts and feelings in me that I haven't experienced in so long I thought they were gone forever. Desire, yes, but more. Appreciation of beauty. A desire for communication, to share my thoughts with another and hear theirs in return. How long has it been since I spoke to another being? Too long to be remembered that's for sure.

I stare at the curtain and wait. Eventually sleep claims me closing the endless circle of my thoughts.

7

JOLIE

*S*ecluded by the bed-curtains, I lie on my back waiting for what happens next. I'm not scared, not really, though maybe I should be. I'm alone with a huge alien-dragon man. I couldn't defend myself against him from anything he wanted to do to me. Which is strangely erotic. My guts tighten and my clit throbs as I consider him taking advantage of me. Of course, I want him to—he's sexy as hell, dominating, and so big. The strength he displays is a huge turn on.

He's also scary. I don't understand why he got angry with me when I didn't want to eat anymore. I was full, but that wasn't good enough for him. Not that I could say that to him. Damn the language barrier is a huge pain! How did Calista deal with this between her and Ladon?

I feel better though. The meat was tasty, wonderful in truth. It had layers of flavor that were rich and enticing. As I chewed it, I felt better, like my body was healing itself or something. Even lying here now, I don't feel the dry scratchiness in the back of my throat or any ache in my muscles.

Holding my hand in front of my face, the tremors that I've grown accustomed to are gone as well.

That drink! Good lord that was insane. It was liquid fire flowing down my throat. I wasn't prepared for something like that. It was the strongest alcohol I've ever had. I liked it though. As the inferno in my stomach took up residence, it sent warmth out to my extremities. It felt like it was flushing away the residual effects of the extreme dehydration of my body.

This planet, I still like calling it Gallifrey, has taken its toll on me. On all of us that haven't taken the epis. But, with the meal Sverre fed me, I almost feel like myself again. Wholly myself, not a shadow I've been trying to hide behind how bad I feel. How much my body aches, the headaches, the nausea that are all symptoms of increasing dehydration. My body just isn't designed for these temperatures.

His is. Damn is it ever. Sverre naked, hmm. Man he looks good. When I woke up with him cuddled next to me, he was so cool and the touch of his scaled skin against mine created silky sensations unlike anything I've ever felt before. The memory comes back and with it the low, pulsing need returns. I need relief. I could have sex with him but no he's not the one. I don't think.

Maybe? When I woke up the room was filled with all those beautiful flowers. They look and smell amazing but the scent of his cooking was the ultimate in sensory experiences. The cooking meat tantalized my nose, making me hungry when before I'd only felt nausea at even the idea of eating.

The way he looked, cooking, the bulk of him doing something so delicate. I imagine him out gathering flowers, picking each one for its size and color. He has a definite eye for color because, as I think about it, the flowers flowed around the room with an aesthetic beauty that points to a definitely practiced eye. He did that for me. Because he'd scared me before.

I don't know a lot about him or his race. Only the tidbits that Calista shared here and there. I know though that Ladon is highly possessive. Calista said something about him calling her his treasure. Considering the things that decorate Sverre's home and the extreme care he is taking with them, it makes sense. Sverre and Ladon both look like dragons, so maybe it's in their genetics to want to hoard things? Could that really be a thing, god knows how many light-years away from earth?

If that's the case then maybe Sverre looks at me as one of his treasures the way Ladon looks at Calista? Hmm, possessed. A treasure, valued, wanted, desired. These thoughts create a warmth in my belly that fills me up. It spreads to my pussy until my clit is a pulsing bundle of needs. Slowly I let my hand drift between my legs. I glance sideways making sure he's not coming closer. I have to lift my head and look to see his silhouette at the table. Good, I need relief.

My hand slides under the hem of the loose pants he gave me and across my dark patch of hair. Being space-wrecked and stranded on an alien planet is hard on personal grooming habits. Pressing my fingers down hard on the top of my opening, I apply pressure to my swollen clit without pulling my folds aside. I don't want to make any noise but I can't stand this.

I press hard and move in a slow circle letting the sensation build. Normally thoughts of different men or movie stars excite me while I masturbate but none of them comes to mind now. All I can think about is Sverre. The coolness of his body. The beautiful color of his scales with the striking blue and yellow accents. The bulk of his muscled chest pulling me tight against him. The feel of his erection pressing against me and how good it would feel to let him slide inside.

My fingers press hard and circle faster. The pulsing tingles increase and my hips grind down against the bed then thrust up. I imagine meeting his hipbones as I go up. The feel of him pushing into my delicate, soft folds, penetrating me to my core. Biting my lip to suppress any sounds I slip my middle finger into my wetness. It passes through my lips causing me to shudder. Circling it slowly now I let my imagination run wild.

Sverre climbs into the bed with me in my mind's eye. His rough, scaled fingers trace lines down along my arms, down my sides, across my breasts. That massive bulge in his pants hangs between us pressing at my opening while he holds himself over me, not penetrating, not yet.

My breath comes in short gasps as my fingers probe deeper and my imagination takes me away.

His lips press against mine. He tastes amazing and, as he lowers his mouth to mine, his body lowers too, pressing his hard member just inside my folds, which part to accommodate his girth. Our tongues seek each other out then dance as we kiss. Holding himself up with one hand, he uses his free hand to tease my breasts.

My nipples are rock hard responding to his imaginary touch. I move my own free hand to my tits and grip each of them in turn while I slide a second finger into my wetness. The pants are limiting my ability to move. I glance quickly over once more, lifting up to make sure he's still occupied at the table, and then slide the pants over my hips. I feel naughty and some kind of dirty knowing I'm doing this with him so close, but at the same time that only makes me more excited.

I run my hand up and down my wet lips without penetrating. I'm so wet it's amazing and the smell of my own sex fills the space making me hornier than ever. I rub quickly up and down, driving myself to new heights of desire.

As I work my hand up and down, I pause at the top each time to give extra pressure on my clitoris. Desire and need build until I'm going crazy with the need to get off.

His cock, so huge, I want to run my hands over his chest as he fills me to my limit with his massive, alien cock. I slide a finger of my right hand into my wetness and use my left to tease circles around my throbbing clitoris.

Slowly I push my finger in and out, just like I imagine he would do if we were fucking. A slow, inexorable drive.

If I struggle, he'd hold me down. My wrists ache softly where he gripped them before. So tight, so strong, and absolutely in control. Remembering that makes me even wetter and my finger slides in to the limit. It's not enough, I want more.

I slip another finger in, then a third, stretching my delicate pink folds. All three slide in easily I'm so wet. I press hard against my clit then circle it fast using all the fingers of my left hand to tease it into higher states of arousal.

My walls are being stretched more than I ever have before and I'm imagining him over me, thrusting, controlling, pinning me down and driving his massive cock into my pussy.

I don't even think about it as my fourth finger slides in. My middle finger finds and grazes around my clit and I'm falling over the edge into an orgasm that's stronger than anything I've ever experienced.

My body tightens, my back arches, my fingers still shove in and out convulsing as I come. My pussy clenches and unclenches.

"Sverre!" I cry out, unable to contain my passion.

The curtain jerks aside with a rattle and he's there. I flush with embarrassment as his turquoise eyes take in my state of disarray and it's obvious what I've been doing. Moving my hands to cover myself I look away unable to meet his eyes. The bulge in his pants stands straight out, searing itself into my memory as I pull my pants over my hips. I turn my back to him hoping he'll go away.

I can't escape and I'm too embarrassed to do anything else.

The curtain closes slowly and then I'm alone with my thoughts and my shame. Why'd I have to call his name? A moan would have been bad enough but no, I had to cry out his name.

What the hell am I doing? What am I going to do? The two questions chase themselves around and around in my mind like a cat chasing its own tail.

8

SVERRE

I try not to think about what I saw or the effect it has on me. The memory of it is crisp and clear. She was beautiful and the scent of her was filling the space. No, I won't press myself on her. She covered herself and turned from me. It's obvious she's not interested in that manner. Maybe in time but not now. She doesn't want me no matter how much I want her.

Food. Food is always a good thing to focus my thoughts with. It's survival. When you focus on survival, it becomes easy to let other things slide away. She'll need more guster meat. What I had might last her three or four days before she'll fall victim again to the ravages of Tajss.

The night passes, and she sleeps or — no, I'll leave my assumption at her sleeping. I don't hear any sounds from the bunk. I'm exhausted and want to lie down myself but I don't want to make things any more awkward than they already are so I doze in my chair. I awake feeling stiff to the sound of movement. My eyes fly open but I calm myself before instincts take over. She's awake and moving quietly around the room.

She moves softly, carefully placing each foot, and it's obvious she's trying not to wake me. After all I've put her through and done, her kindness strikes into my heart like a bolt. Even with the slips I've had to bijass, my primal needs and desires, she still cares about me and wants to let me sleep. My smile parts my lips while I watch her. I shift my foot to draw her attention without startling her. She looks over quickly, her eyes wide then she smiles broadly when she sees I'm awake.

She raises her right hand in front of herself and motions it side to side saying rapid words. Her voice is musical as always but there's an extra note of brightness to it this morning. Or perhaps it's my own imagination and sincere hope that she has forgiven me for my intrusion on her privacy last night. When she called my name, I thought something was wrong. I keep my home safe as possible but there are things that still invade on occasion and even if small, they're still deadly.

Of course, what I found was anything but a dangerous situation. Or maybe it was. It might be the most dangerous situation I've faced in years. The sensations and feelings she awakens in me are best left dormant. What right do I have to happiness? She walks closer as she talks which pushes aside my morose thoughts. Her smile lifts me up and I feel alive. I have to go hunting today, but I want her to stay. I spent a large portion of the night working on a way to make her understand. Now to see if my plan works.

"Jj-oo-lee," I say then smile and motion to the chair across from me.

She looks up at me with an energy and vibrancy that makes her seem bouncy. One of her eyebrows arches up then she shrugs her shoulders and takes the seat. Good, I'm off to a good start. I gathered some small objects last night which I have sitting at the side of the table ready to use. She watches me expectantly as I take a deep breath then pull the objects closer. I hold up a large, polished red oblong rock between us.

"Sverre," I say motioning the rock towards myself.

I set it on the table and repeat my name while pointing at the rock then myself. She cocks her head to one side then laughs.

"Sverre?" she makes it a question as she points at the rock then at me.

I nod. We're off to a good start. Grabbing the next object, which is a clear piece of glass that is much smaller with smooth edges. The curves of it made me think of her so I chose it as the representation. I hold it up in the same manner between us.

"Jj-oo-lee," I say motioning the piece towards her.

I repeat what I did with the last one and she does the same so I feel certain she understands my goal. Grabbing the small box for my next representation, I set it down beside the two objects representing us.

"Home," I say pointing at the box then motioning around the room.

This one takes a while because it's a new word. She starts out mimicking the sound and at last I get up and walk around the room patting the walls, then going back to the box and patting the inside walls of it. It takes some time but finally she says home in my own language and smiles broadly. I think she understands at least. I grab a knife, hold it up, this I think she understands because she says a word almost immediately.

I work out the word she is saying. There are too many soft sounds in her language. It's difficult to sound them out correctly but I get it at last. When I do she jumps out of her chair and bounces on the balls of her feet talking swiftly.

"Knife," I repeat, carefully sounding out the word.

She resumes her seat and I go back to explaining my plan. Next, I grab a small pile of pebbles. I hold them out in my palm then place them on the table.

"Food," I say in her language pointing to them. She nods her understanding.

Now for the important part.

"Jj-oo-lee," I say while picking up the glass representing her and place it in the box while looking pointedly at her.

Then I take the knife and the stone representing me in one hand I move them away from the box and mime stabbing the food pebbles. "Sverre," I say.

She looks from my hands to my eyes then back again as her mouth forms an O then she starts shaking her head violently side to side. She says a word, points, then says the same word again.

"No?" I make it a question as I try to sound it out.

"No," she says pointing at my representations.

"Food," I say pointing to my mouth then belly again.

She frowns then grabs the glass representing her, takes it out of the box, and places it beside my hand that is holding the knife and rock of me. Then she nods her head up and down smiling saying a different word. I listen to the word closely and she repeats it while pointing.

"Yessssss," I say mimicking it.

She nods more and repeats the word.

"Yes!" she says emphatically pointing at the glass then at my hand containing the knife and the rock of me.

Frowning, I try to come up with a way to argue. Some way to communicate how dangerous any hunt is. I can't put her at risk. I don't know I can protect her while I'm hunting and not end up with both of us hurt or worse. At last, I take the piece of glass and lay it on the table. I lay down the rock representing me and move it close to the herd pebbles with the knife beside it. Then I sweep the pebbles towards her glass covering it over. Pointing I shake my head side to side as I've seen her do.

She shrugs and shakes her head as well. She uncovers the glass and smiles as she places it next to the rock. She points to me then to her as if that says it all. I'm losing my carefully planned argument. I try different ways of making the danger clear but the more I work at it the more clear it becomes to me that she doesn't care. She's not going to be left behind. When I put her back in the box, she picks the glass up and mimes following after me. That would be worse than anything I can imagine. My territory is filled with hidden dangers I'm sure she's not prepared to deal with. As I come to realize that's fully what she intends to do if I don't take her with me I give in.

Resigning myself to her accompanying me on the hunt, I put away the objects then prepare. A pack I use to carry essentials lies next to the table, so I grab it then fill it with supplies for a night away from home. After double checking everything is ready, I get my lochaber. I check its edge to make sure it's sharp then oil the wooden handle. In my chest, I find a couple of blanket rolls, which I tie to the pack, then I'm ready to go.

Jolie helps as she can but this is routine for me and I do most of it alone. Satisfied at last I look from the door to her. I point at her then the bed and tilt my head hoping that maybe she'll capitulate and decide to stay after all. She grins and shakes her head, not that I expected anything different. Maybe this hunt will be easy. I hope so. Walking out the door then up the entrance passage, I slide the rock aside that hides my home and we emerge into the burning light.

My protective lenses close while she shields her eyes from the much brighter light of the sun. Once the rock is back over the entrance, I shift the sand to make sure it's not obvious, then point in the direction I want to go. She smiles, and we set off. It isn't long before I spot the tracks of a herd of bivo. She didn't do well with the smoked and dried meat but fresh it should be good for her.

She doesn't move as fast as I do. I didn't think of how much it would slow me down making sure she could keep up. The sun is dropping low by the time we catch up to the herd. When I spot them, I drop to the ground and motion for her to do the same. We hide behind a huge boulder and watch the herd. They mewl as they move their large heads and tusks, digging through the sand to stir up anything edible. Small animals, hidden plants, anything that will fill their bellies and keep them moving.

One of the bivo has fallen behind. It's old and weak, judging from the way it moves. As we watch, it falls further behind the herd, which is drifting closer to the ridge. I couldn't have asked for a better situation. I meet Jolie's eyes, hold my palm flat, and motion towards the ground then point up at the ridge. She nods, so I lie flat and crawl towards the ridge. Pausing to check on her, I see she's mimicking me well, so I keep moving.

At the top of the ridge, I crawl to the edge and look down. The drop is about twenty feet, which is good. Enough for me to get extra force as I come down but not too much for my wings to handle. The majority of the herd has moved past the ridge with only a few stragglers left behind. Jolie crawls up next to me and looks over the edge. The concern is obvious on her face.

"Jj-oo-lee," I say softly then pat the ground trying to indicate for her to stay put.

When she smiles, I take it for understanding and smile back. I rise up, gripping the lochaber in both hands, and spread my wings in preparation. The lone, straggling bivo below stops as my shadow falls over it, and it mewls. Its massive head looks side-to-side but isn't able to look up, where the real threat is. I leap, holding my lochaber before me point down. The point drives in true just behind the bivo's massive head, severing its spine and killing it instantly.

Folding my wings as it falls under me; I jerk the lochaber free, then crouch and look around. The herd continues grazing, paying no mind to the lost weak one. You can't be too careful in hunting bivo. One or even two aren't difficult, but if you get in the middle of a herd, they will trample and gore you. In a herd, they're very dangerous. Looking up, I can see Jolie peering down over the edge of the ridge with her eyes wide.

"Jj-oo-lee," I say softly, holding up a hand to indicate I want her to stay there.

The herd is still close and I don't want to risk her attracting their attention. They move away and, once they're out of my sight, I motion for her to join me. Her head disappears from the ridge and while she's walking down and around, I dress the meat and harvest what I want from it. I'm almost done when she comes around the corner. When she arrives, she quickly sees what I'm doing and jumps in to help. As I butcher the meat, she wraps the pieces in my oilcloth and then puts them away in my pack.

The sun is setting by the time we finish and there's too much fresh blood here to make this a good camping spot. We gather up our things and I gesture that we should go. She falls in beside me and I match my stride to hers. She talks almost non-stop as we walk. I remain silent, simply enjoying her voice. Once I'm sure we've put enough distance between us and the spilled blood, I stop to make a camp.

I untie the blankets and lay them out for each of us. Then I remove some firewood and tinder from the pack. I use my throat glands to start a fire, which Jolie seems to find fascinating. She motions with wide eyes until I create fire again.

I'm not sure why this fascinates her but, apparently, it's not an ability she has.

Once the fire is going, I take out some of the meat and impale it on skewers. I push the end of each skewer into the ground so that the meat is sizzling in the flames. She continues talking, each of us sitting on our blankets. I watch her, so mesmerized I almost forget to turn the meat. The way she moves, the cascade of fur on her head that sometimes falls across her forehead, everything about her is beautiful. She moves with a grace that is unlike anything I've ever seen. So much energy and vibrancy contained in the small package of her body. In my eyes, I can see her fairly vibrating even when she's sitting still.

The meat cooks and then we eat. This time it goes much better. She's able to eat it and keep it down well. Good, the guster meat has helped. It bought me time to figure out a way to get her epis. We lie on the blankets, which she stays on top of even as the temperature drops. To me, once the sun goes down it gets quite cold but, apparently, it's still too hot for her body. Jolie tosses and turns, then stands up, grabs her blanket, and comes over to lie next to me. She cuddles up close, pressing her body against mine.

The warmth of her is pleasing and arousing. My cock stiffens and my thoughts turn carnal. She rests her head on her arm and makes no indication that she desires more than my body's cooling ability. Though I want so much more from her, I won't take it. She has to initiate anything further between us. I will hold the line between the man and the primal urge that threatens to consume me.

9

JOLIE

*W*aking up slowly, I realize how much I like the way we fit together. His strong arm lies across my waist and curls up over my breasts. He's so much bigger than me. I'm curled inside the C shape of his body. It makes me feel safe. I roll to face him and find he's already awake and watching me.

"Good morning!" I say cheerful. "Man, what I wouldn't give for some coffee. Mornings just aren't right without coffee."

It's clear he doesn't understand me but he smiles and stands. I help gather our blankets and roll them. He gathers up the pack, says something, then starts walking, so I follow.

"So this language thing is tough. How do I tell you I really need to get back to my friends? It's pretty important, I think, at this point that I get back. They're going to be missing me. I guess that raises the question why you live way out here? You found me at the city, so why don't you live there? Ladon's nice, you two would get along I think. Maybe. Or maybe not? Is that why you live way out here, wherever here is?"

He glances at me as I talk but remains silent. I've grown

use to his long silences, and it's not like we're actually talking, anyway. I mean he's there and I'm here but we're not communicating. Exchanging actual ideas. That takes a lot of gesturing and meticulous role-play to get our points across to each other. The play he put on when he wanted me to stay behind brings a smile to my face. He's so sweet.

It wasn't hard to figure out what he wanted because he was worried I'd get hurt but to hell with that! This has been a grand adventure. Well actually, this has been a lot of walking and then lying on the sand watching him kill a big beast, but it still beats waiting alone in a cavern not knowing if he would come back. No, this has been fun. I like him. I like the way he looks at me and doesn't say much. It's nice. When he does act, he's strong and certain which has an appeal I've never thought about before.

The men I knew before, on the ship, weren't like that. They were all, hmm, I don't know a good word for it. Soft, I guess. The hardest decision life on the ship required you to make was whether to go out for dinner or eat at home. Our lives were incredibly routine and predictable. I mean the day you were born your job and education were set before you could say "Mama." It's the way it had to be on a generation ship. You couldn't have some people decide not to do the jobs they were designed to do. The ship wouldn't survive, and we'd never have reached our destination with a viable colony.

So yeah, those men weren't manly men. The movies and television shows from earth had man's man types. Clint Eastwood, John Wayne. But Doctor Who was always more my type. Smart and in control. I see some of that in Sverre now that I think of it. He's big, much too big and bulky to be a Doctor but it's in the way he plans things out. He's smart and uses his mind as much as his muscles. From what I've seen of

Ladon he muscles his way through everything but not Sverre.

This is all just a fantasy in my head to pass the time. I can't let myself get so caught up. Sverre is way ahead of me and off to my left. Realizing I've fallen behind, I take off running. If I cut across diagonal, I'll reach him faster so I do that. On my third step, the ground shifts and then I'm falling.

"HELP!" I yell as the sand sucks me down. Blackness yawns below.

My stomach clenches tight as the sensation of empty space opens up and I'm falling. Screeching sounds are followed by rustling leather then things are flying at me out of the dark and I scream. I scream so hard it feels like my throat rips but I keep right on yelling. Things, big nasty things, are hitting me and I'm still falling. I look up towards the receding light reaching in vain for something to grab on to.

"Jj-oo-leeeee!" Sverre yells, appearing above me with his wings spread, diving in for me.

My heart leaps as I reach for him, hoping against hope. He closes his wings to his body, and then he's plummeting closer. Shapes that I can't see clearly fly at him, screeching. I catch glimpses of wings, teeth, and green flashing eyes. They tear at his flesh as he closes with me. When he's close, he opens his arms wide, then grabs me tight. His wings pop open, breaking our fall. Then we hit the ground and we're tumbling head over heels. He's wrapped around me in a protective ball, and I'm still screaming in fear and relief.

As we roll to a stop, he leaps to his feet. The weapon he used yesterday drops to his hand. I start to stand but he pushes me down to the ground then stands straddled over me. The flapping of wings and the screeching continues. He turns side to side, waiting, then the things dive out of the blackness, attacking him. He swings and one of them is sliced in half, but two more hit him from the other side and sink their teeth in.

He grabs one with his free hand, ripping it away, and slams it to the ground where he then impales it with his weapon. Two more dive in, but these he ducks. Grabbing the one still chewing on him, he throws it off and stabs it. He stumbles and almost falls. I don't see any severe damage, but the wounds he does have are affecting him.

"Sverre!" I cry out as another one comes at his back.

He whirls around with his weapon and hits it like a bat connecting with a baseball. It's flung into the darkness and I hear it smack against a wall. He wavers once again and fear knots my guts. The sounds of the things are growing less. There can't be more than two or three of them left. I rise up to my knees behind Sverre so I can try to help protect his back. I don't know with what, or how, but I have to help him. He dove here to save me and I have to repay that kindness.

Two of the things swoop by overhead, dodging in and out of the light streaming down from the hole above us. It's only ten or fifteen feet but, when I was falling, it felt like miles. Sverre turns a circle with his weapon at the ready. Our backs are pressed against each other and I notice that there's a tremor running through him. He's shaking like his muscles are spasming. One of the creatures screeches and dives in, only to meet its end on his weapon. The other one flies out of the hole above us screeching. Now it's quiet. Sverre completes one more circle then his knees give out, and he drops to the floor.

"Sverre!" I call.

He looks up at me from his hands and knees. The muscles of his back are spasming so hard I can see them jumping under the cloth. His arms are shaking and he can barely raise his head to look at me. He raises a hand towards me then the spasms reach the arm supporting him and he falls to his face.

"No!" I grab his shoulder and try to lift.

He's heavy, forcing me to strain as I try to turn him over. He moves, trying to help, but his muscles all quiver with hard spasms that make me hurt watching them. I get him on to his side and he looks at me with pain in his beautiful eyes. His body convulses hard, throwing him over onto his back. He's shaking, legs kicking, arms flailing, and then his eyes close. He goes still.

"No, no, no," I say over and over, a mantra against the worst.

Holding my ear next to his mouth, I hear the soft intake of air. He's breathing. Thank god! I lay my head on his chest and listen. His heart is beating, but it's odd. There's an echo to it that isn't right. But, for now, I'm going with the fact it's beating at all. The sun streams down from the opening I fell through, creating a circle of light that's burning hot. When I touch his face and arms, they're warm. I don't know if they're too warm or not. His body handles the heat of this planet better than mine does, but what does he need? The heat is making me uncomfortable so I decide to move him.

Crouching by his head, I hook him under his shoulders and try to drag him past the circle of light. He doesn't budge, so I dig my heels in and lean back with all my weight. My feet sink into the sand up to my ankles then finally he slides a few inches, far enough that I land on my ass. I reposition myself, hook him again, and repeat the process. I have to do this five separate times before I finally pull him just outside the streaming light.

Moving into the shade lets me see into the shadows and gives me the layout of the cavern I fell into. It looks like an old tunnel of some kind. Now that the things that attacked us are gone, it's empty. It continues to my left and right as far as the light will allow me to see before blackness swallows it. The walls are smooth as is the floor and ceiling, like it was

bored out by a machine. It's too smooth to have been naturally formed.

Sverre's chest rises and falls slowly but he doesn't move so
I inspect him for wounds. I find several bites, each of them
inflamed and swollen. The worst are the ones on his back
where he had to tear the things off. They took chunks of his
flesh with them leaving open wounds.

He packed for the hunt and I wonder if there's not something of medicinal value in there. He seems so thoughtful
and careful that it seems likely there'd be something. I dig
through his pack and, almost at the bottom, I find a jar which
is wrapped in oil cloth tied off with a string. When I remove
the lid, there's a thick, goopy salve inside that smells incredibly strong. The odor of it assaults my senses making my
eyes water and my sinuses burn.

Seems like medicine to me, so I dip my fingers in. It's cool
at first touch but warms on my fingers as I uncover the first
of the bites and smear it over the angry-looking tear in his
skin. I treat each wound carefully with the salve until I'm
sure I have each of them covered. I don't have any bandages
to cover them, so I use his shirt and pants to keep the salve
from collecting dirt. Once I'm finished, I re-wrap the jar and
return it to the bag along with all the supplies.

Now I wait. The adrenaline has dropped out of my
system leaving me feeling drained clear down to my bones.
I've got nothing left and I'm thirsty. Sverre had a water skin.
Wearily, I climb to my feet and look for it. I find it a few feet
away lying in a pool of wetness. It hit a sharp rock when it
landed and was cut open. All the water is soaking into the
sand. Looking at the diminishing wet spot the urge to cry is
overwhelming but I'm too dry for tears. Dry sobs shake my
body for a few minutes. When it passes, I return to Sverre
and lie down beside him.

I'm beyond exhaustion. I just want to curl up with him

and go to sleep. I want his arms around me, holding me tight against his cool, strong body. He's a stranger to me. I don't know him and we can't communicate, but he's done more for me in the time we've been together than any of the guys I ever dated.

Lying here with my head on his shoulder, listening to the soft sound of his labored breathing I realize how scared I am. What if he doesn't wake up? It's about more than my own survival. I like him. I want him to be okay. Sure, I'm screwed if he doesn't wake up, but I could survive. I'm smart. I can probably figure out how to get out of here. Honestly? I don't know if I want to without him. His strength and dominating nature is balanced by how kind and thoughtful he is. He makes me feel... happy? Safe? Cared for? Maybe something more?

Is this how it was for you, Calista? Did you fall for Ladon like this?

Darkness claims me as my thoughts spin wildly out of control.

10

SVERRE

*L*ooking around the council table, I see they're all in agreement. When I riserise to my feet, it feels as though the air is thick, resisting my motion, like it's trying to tell me to stay seated.

Someone screams my name. She's falling.

No, no, this is now. I'm at the council. We're about to vote. The debate is over. Once I stand, I'll call for it, and then everything will go to hell. It's wrong; we're making the wrong choice. How do I tell them? I have to convince them.

She's screaming my name, I need to reach her. She's falling.

I shake my head to clear it of the distant scream. My duty is clear, and this is the right choice. Revolt is the only answer. We cannot let our people continue under the yoke of the Star Imperiya. I make it to my feet and meet the eyes of each member of the council. They're resolved. We are resolved.

Jolie. Jolie is screaming.

Who... Why is she screaming my name? The room wavers in and out around me. Darkness encroaches from the sides. None of the council members seems to notice. They pound the table with their hands as I stand but then the darkness covers them over. The

79

table is slowly engulfed until only blackness surrounds me. I'm alone. Alone as I've always been. It's what I deserve.

No, I have to see. Must open my eyes, must....

MY EYES SNAP OPEN AND I GASP IN A DEEP BREATH, LOOKING wildly around as I get my bearings. A tunnel. I'm in a tunnel, where? Jolie! She's beside me. My treasure, my greatest prize lies unmoving. I gently shake her but she doesn't open her eyes.

"Jj-oo-lee," I yell, and her name echoes off the walls of the zemlja tunnel, but still she doesn't respond.

Her skin is bright red, like it was when I found her. I know she's overheating, which means the guster meat has worn off. I thought it would last longer, but the restorative properties must have been weakened from being stored too long. Damn it! What do I do now? The sun streams in from the hole above us, illuminating the tunnel. Jolie's skin is blistering as the light falls on her. I need to cool her down, but staying in this tunnel is not an option. The zemlja sometimes travel back the way they've come, and at the very least it means that one has been through here and might still be in the area. I don't want to confront one on its home turf.

I sling the pack over my shoulder, then gather her in my arms. She stirs and trembles but doesn't wake. I don't have enough water to cool her and home is still a day's journey away. There's an oasis closer to where we are that will have water, so I decide to head there. The first problem will be getting out of this tunnel without running into the thing that created it or any more sismis. The flying monsters stay out of the heat during the day and emerge at night to hunt. Their bite is poisonous but not fatal, except in large doses. I must have taken enough bites to knock me out, leaving Jolie on her own.

She's so light. Carrying her is almost like having nothing in my arms. She's a waif of a girl, nothing like the women of my own race. Her soft curves, the strange places she has fur, the smell of her, and the way so much of her is unprotected is so different. No shielding bone or scales to keep her reproductive parts from harm. Her home world must be very different from mine. She's not built to handle this harsh environment.

How do I get us out of here? She convulses while I debate. I must make a decision. Every passing moment is one step closer to her not waking at all. If I don't get her body core temperature down, she'll die. That cannot happen. I won't allow it! The opening above us is not that far. Alone with the use of my wings I could get out of it easily.

Can I do it carrying her? There's only one way to find out. I move a few feet from the hole to give myself a running start. Mentally I brace myself, then run and pop my wings just before I'm under the hole. Flapping them with all my strength, I leap. They catch air, and I'm climbing, holding the height gained by my leap. My head rises just above the opening. I reach out for the edge with one hand, but Jolie spasms in my arms, shifting her weight. She's sliding, and I'm going to drop her if I don't do something. I'll grab her with the arm I was reaching with.

I coast to the ground and land with a thump. The muscles of my wings ache from the exertion. This isn't going to work. Lying Jolie down, gently out of the direct sun, I pace the length of the tunnel as far as the light will let me see in each direction. If the sismis were living in here, there has to be an exit that they used. The problem is that it could be quite a ways away in either direction.

Is that a hint of air flowing from this direction? I walk a little further into the darkness but can't decide. As I pace back, I examine the tunnel for something, anything that I can use to get us out of here. There has to be a way. Possibilities race through my thoughts. Every possible plan ends in a question leaving me with no answers. There is no clear-cut way forward.

Behind the fog of my memories, creeping fear crawls forward. Everything rides on my success. I don't want to imagine a life without her now that I have her. She has to live. There are similarities here to the past, but that past is buried behind the bijass. More, I don't want to remember. I don't want to know because deep down, I know it's all my fault. This time will be different. I will make it different.

Gathering her into my arms, I cradle her gently. My treasure, your voice will fill the air with its sweet music soon. I will save you.

I look left then right and make my choice. I head left where I thought the air came from, running as fast as I can. I spread my wings and use them to lighten my weight. They ache, badly, and every third step there's a sharp pain but I push past it. It doesn't matter if it hurts. All that matters is her. She shakes in my arms, her muscles convulsing, and she moans so I adjust her as she squirms in my hold.

I don't stop. I'm committed to a path forward, and it has to work. As I run, I study the tunnel looking for any sign of a way out. There has to be one or the sismis would not have been here. As I run, the light dims until I'm in complete darkness. My eyes adjust down to the infrared spectrum until I'm seeing only the outlines of things. The roof of the tunnel is bright, thanks to the heat of the sun warming this far down into the ground, and it gives me enough to see by.

I run for what feels like hours. There's no way to measure the time down here. One step after another. Exhaustion hits my muscles, and each step takes all the effort I can muster to make it but I push on. There is no time to slow down. She moans and shakes more as I run. Each time she moans, my stomach clenches into a tight knot. I have to save her.

The roof of the tunnel grows brighter then I feel a warm breeze. Hope blossoms and I run with renewed vigor. It's not long before I see a light ahead. When I reach it there's a slight angle up and a hole that is within my reach. The sun is still streaming in, so it's not nightfall yet.

The tunnel continues but the zemlja that created it went above ground here, and the way ahead has partially collapsed into a pile of rubble. I could pull myself out since it's within reach, but the rubble makes it so I can take her with me easily. I climb up onto the shifting sand and rock, and find a stable place to stand. Crouching down with Jolie held tight to my chest, I fold my wings, summon all my strength, and leap. I clear the opening, spread my wings, and flap them to make sure I gain enough height. My muscles protest the strain, but I catch the wind. I glide over to land by the opening. I clear the hole when some of the cartilage in my left wing tears, and it collapses, useless.

Jolie and I tumble to the ground. I tuck into a ball around her, taking the brunt of the fall. When we come to a stop, I uncurl and make sure she wasn't hurt. She looks no worse for the wear. My biceps are shaking as I pick her back up, but I lift her despite the exhaustion.

Turning in a slow circle to get my bearings, I spot an oasis. There to the west is a landmark I recognize. We came out a bit further along than I planned to make it but it's in the direction of the city where the others like her are. Closer to that other Zmaj's territory. The bijass flares as I think of entering his territory again. There isn't a choice. I'll have to face him, and we'll have to come to terms. I'll do it for her. He'll comply when he understands, I'm sure. I have to find a way to make it happen. She's worth it.

Jolie moans softly, and I push aside those concerns for

later. Now she needs water. I can't run because my left wing is worthless. Without it, the sand pulls at me with each step I take. It makes the journey to the oasis take twice as long as it should and I curse each step. The sun beats down, but nothing else interferes. When I get to the edge of the oasis, I stop just within the shade cast by the outermost baobabaoba trees and lay Jolie down. I draw my lochaber and approach the oasis in a defensive stance.

An oasis draws all the predators of Tajss. Some call them home, the deadly cvet plants that will eat a Zmaj, or any other creature, and the majmun primates that live in packs in the trees. Others stop for the water or to hunt the majmun like the guster who will eat anything.

This oasis is large, big enough I can't see the far side and the ends to either side are hundreds of yards away. As I move in slowly, some of the foliage ahead rustles and I prepare to attack. Moving closer, lochaber at the ready, the rustling stops. I wait for three beats of my hearts to see if anything emerges. Nothing comes out so I move closer until I'm close enough to part the leaves with my lochaber.

On the far side of the leaves is a tiny cvet, a seedling at most. Cvet grow to be huge flowers with long leaves that spread out from a pretty, yellow center. The center is a mouth and, between the leaves, vines grow to trap prey and pull it in. The leaves are sharp edged and have a paralytic poison that immobilizes what it captures. This one is just big enough to eat rodents or a bird. I don't want to risk anything though, so I get close enough, then stab it through its open mouth, driving my lochaber through and into the ground. It screeches, shudders, then dies.

Inspecting the rest of the immediate area, I find no other threats, so I pick up Jolie and bring her close. I gather fallen limbs and leaves to build a shelter that will shield her from the sun. Once she's safely inside, I go over to the edge of the water and fill my bottle. I return to her and strip her of her clothing, then slowly pour the water over her. She shudders, twists, then moans as the cool water covers her red and blistered skin. The redness recedes as I continue getting more water and pouring it.

Once her breathing becomes deeper, and her skin is less of a red tone and more of its natural yellow tan, I stop with the water. Then I strip down and lie next to her, letting my body naturally pull the heat from her and disperse it. The scent of her hair, the curve of her body as I adjust her to press more of her flesh against mine, the softness of her where I would expect there to be hard protection is erotic. My prime penis hardens uncomfortably, but its being pressed between us pleases me. I wrap my arms around her and wait.

Once she's able, we'll travel to the city and her people. Until then, I will enjoy the sensations of her pressing against me and feel glad that she is safe. My decision was the right one. I saved her and that is enough, for now.

11

JOLIE

I wake up slowly. Every muscle in my body hurts. I'm exhausted and so dry that my mouth feels like the sand that makes up this damn planet I'm stuck on. Awareness returns slowly and I don't want it so I try to escape back into the blackness of sleep but I can't.

I'm not hot. That's the first thing that I really become aware of once I accept that I'm going to be awake. That's such a relief that I bask in it for a moment. Only then do I become aware of Sverre pressing up against me with his massive manhood trapped between our bodies. Desire blooms like an opening flower as soon as I realize it.

He saved me. I've been holding out for a man who would care for me, someone who would look at me like Ladon looks at Calista. His arm holds me close against his cool skin. Our bodies are melded together, and yet he didn't take advantage of me. He could have and his body is making it plain he wants to. A slow smile spreads across my face with an unstoppable force as my chest expands with a light, airy feeling. I shift, enjoying the feeling of his cock pressing against me, then I roll over towards him.

His eyes are open and he's watching me. I touch his face and trace the line of his jaw. He says something, then smiles. His fingertips trail down my spine, and I shiver as sensations rocket through my nerves. Wetness grows between my legs and I want him. He's mine and I'm going to give myself to him.

"Good morning," I say. "We can't communicate but I want you to know something. I care about you. I like the way you look at me. I wasn't sure, I was scared, I think, but you've always treated me with respect and care. Even when you're being kind of big and scary, you're still kind."

He says something that of course I don't understand but, at the end of it, he says my name. He places a hand on my chest, resting it on my heart. He must see I don't understand because he takes my hand and places it on his chest where I can feel the beating of his own heart.

"Jj-oo-lee," he repeats.

My smile feels like it's pouring out from my soul. I scoot closer then lean in and kiss him. His lips are cool against mine but softer than I imagined they would be. His tongue grazes my lips then gently slides past them until my tongue meets his. I melt into him with that kiss.

Putting a hand on his shoulder, I push and he rolls with my small effort. I break the kiss and lean back admiring the hard, scaled muscles of his body. The colors of his scales are beautiful, glinting with reflected sunlight, sharp blues and yellows that accent his turquoise eyes. The rise and fall of his chest shifts the light creating a changing pattern of beauty. I let my fingers trail along his muscled chest and across his hard stomach.

His cock is big and strange. Unbelievably huge with ridges running the length of him. If Calista hadn't already had sex with Ladon, I'd be worried but I know it will work. Throwing my leg over the top of him, I sit on his stomach and run my hands across his beautiful body. He talks as his hands find my breasts, and with surprising gentleness, he kneads them.

When I trace the lines of his jaw down and across his neck, the sensations of his scales and skin under my fingers is electric. I slide back so his erection presses against me and he hisses. I kiss him again as my hands roam down the muscles of his arms. He wraps his arms around me, letting his fingers trail down my spine to my ass, then brings his hands to rest on my hips.

I'm wet, soaking wet, but still nervous. He lifts his hips trying to roll us over but I want to be in control so I resist, shaking my head from side to side. He stops then and lies back, giving me control.

Reaching behind myself, I take hold of his cock. It's so strange and alien that it makes butterflies dance in my stomach again. It's big and has ridges that run along the top down to his pelvis. I stroke up and down his shaft and he moans. His hands tighten on my hips pulling on my ass. I slide back so his cock is between my cheeks and then slowly rise up.

His eyes roll up in his head and a smile of pure bliss spreads across his lips. I rise up then scoot back while shifting my grip on his cock. I lower myself until it's at my opening, ready for penetration. I take several deep breaths before lowering any further. He's watching me and I can see the concern in his eyes. I smile reassuringly with a confidence I don't really feel, but I want this.

I lower and the head of his dick spreads my soft, delicate folds. The tip alone is bigger than I've ever experienced before. The first ridge slides through and the phrase 'ribbed for her pleasure' makes so much more sense to me now. Wetness flows down his shaft. His cock inside becomes more comfortable so I resume the downward pressure.

My eyes go wide with surprise. Biting my lip, I hold myself up, once more giving time for my body to grow accustomed to his girth. It feels so good already. Better than anything I've ever had and we haven't even begun yet. As my body adjusts, I slide down to the next ridge.

"Mmmm," I moan.

Desire demands satisfaction. My body wants this badly. My thighs quiver with pleasure to the point they become weak. In a sudden loss of control, I slide fully onto his massive shaft in a single, fast motion that overwhelms my mind completely with a flood of sensations. I cry out in surprise and pleasure, and Sverre beneath me gasps then moans.

I'm filled beyond anything I've ever felt. The ridges press against my insides and against my clit causing an electrical storm in the core of my body. The sensations carry me away and I'm over the edge to an orgasm.

It rips through me and my back arches which rubs my throbbing clitoris against the ridge at the base of his cock, driving me deeper still into the throes of my orgasm.

"SVERRE!"

My hands claw mindlessly at his chest. Stars fill my vision. Nothing has ever felt this good. My skin tingles as the orgasm passes. With every shift of my hips, my over-sensitive clit rubs against the ridge on his pelvis.

I'm panting and he's holding me still by my waist. Leaning down, I kiss him. He returns my kiss. Soft, gentle, and loving. He slowly moves his hips in a circular motion. His cock inside me rotates, and the protrusion grinds against me again. A slow build of fresh passion and desire rises.

The final shudders of my last orgasm release in a shiver down my spine then I'm building to new heights. My hands run across his hard muscles, while his run up and down my spine, grab my ass and tease the sides of my breasts. My nipples drag along the rough scales on his chest. He changes his rhythm, moving his hips in a circle then up at the end, so his cock is driven deeper inside. I feel it hitting bottom as I'm expanded out. He twines a hand in my hair holding me tight against him.

He hisses then moans into our kiss. We stop kissing, our heads resting on each other's shoulders as we grind against each other. He holds me tight against his chest, grinding faster, moaning louder, then he calls out my name with a long hiss.

"Jjj-ooo-leeeeeeeee," he cries, thrusting up and holding.

His cock expands inside me then I feel it pumping his seed. As soon as it expands, a fresh orgasm takes me into its embrace. I'm washed away like a leaf on a river. He holds me tight as we come together.

Rising up onto my arms, I meet his eyes and we kiss. His cock is softening but still feels massive. Even soft, it's bigger than any cock I've ever seen.

I rise to lie down beside him, resting my head on his shoulder. He trails his fingers along my backside and I trace the scales on his chest as my breathing slows to normal. His fingers leave trails of fire across my skin. I'm satisfied. Deep and fully satisfied. His massive cock, now soft lying against him, moves and pulls back but as it does a second cock rises and stands erect.

"What the hell!" I exclaim, rising up on my elbow with my eyes wide in surprise.

He tilts his head to the side quizzically. I point at his now-erect second cock. He shakes his head, not understanding. He's an alien, what did I expect? Well, obviously not two cocks, but damn. Looking at that hard member saluting the sky makes desire roar into a fresh bonfire of flames that threaten to consume me. He moves and rises, rolling so that he's over me now.

He kisses me gently while lowering his hips. As we kiss, he slides his cock in. Pleasure sweeps through my body as each ridge of his cock passes through forcing me wider and my body grips him tightly. He slides in until the base ridge is pressing hard on my tightly wound clit. He rotates his hips, and a moan escapes me.

Once he's fully in, he retreats, slowly, making sure his cock touches every nerve of my tight pussy as he pulls back. He leaves the head and first ridge inside on his retreat then thrusts straight back in. He cries out my name again as he penetrates. I claw at his back, holding on to the base of his wings. It's amazing. I'm blown away, and I know it won't be long before this carries me to yet another orgasm.

We move in time with each other. Each thrust in I rise to meet and each retreat I pull back as well. We drive together like the crashing of the waves against a beach. It hits suddenly. I'm swept away as he thrusts in and then he holds, throwing his head back.

"Jj-oo-lleee!" he cries out to the sky.

He holds his massive, ridged cock deep inside. The protrusion on his pelvis places a constant pressure against my clit. My back arches; my toes curl; even the hair on my head tingles as every nerve of my body alights under the electrical storm that is raging through me.

He lowers himself down and kisses me. Soft, gentle kisses, his hard cock still inside. Our tongues dance together in a light minuet until the last of the orgasmic storm passes. Only then does he pull back. We cuddle up next to each other and, in moments, I'm asleep.

12

SVERRE

*J*olie stirs in her sleep. She's beautiful, and she's mine. She chose me as I hoped she would. I waited, and she chose; now we will be as one. Pride and joy fill me as I watch her sleep in the makeshift shelter I built for her. As soon as she fell asleep the night before I slid out to stand guard. The sun is on the horizon now. The first hints of red rays break across the distant sand dunes and rocks.

We're not far from the city. A few days at most. I hope that I can come to terms with the other Zmaj there. She needs epis, and I can't get it alone. I'll need his help to gather enough to save her. How far gone to bijass is he? There is no choice but to confront him and find out. Instinct screams at me that this is a bad idea, but if I don't there's no way I can give her any quality of life. Her body has to adjust to the planet if her life is to be anything more than a constant struggle against dehydration.

She stirs, stretches, then her eyes snap open. She looks out and smiles which I return. When she climbs out, I offer her some food. She stands and stretches and my eyes trace the lines of her beautiful body. She's amazing, sensual, and beautiful. My cock stirs but there is no time for that. At least not now. Once she's safe, there will be plenty of time. She pulls the last of her clothes back on and then talks rapidly. I lose myself in the music of her voice. She walks over and puts a hand on my chest, and it's like fire touching me. All my senses go to that point of contact, memorizing each sensation.

She smiles and my heart lifts. Placing my hand over hers, I lean in and kiss her. She is everything I've ever dreamed of. Placing a hand on her stomach, I flatten it out against her.

"Baby," I say.

Her brow furrows. She shakes her head and says something. I repeat the word and she starts mimicking my word until at last she gets it and I nod. I move my hand out from her stomach miming her belly growing with a child we create. I want a family with her. Nothing could make my life more complete. Raising our child together is more than I could have ever hoped for before. She brings that light into my world.

As I mime and repeat the word, her eyes widen and she says something. I listen carefully as she repeats the word then I mimic it back to her. Her mouth tightens into a hard line and she shakes her head then looks into the distance. She's thinking so I give her the time she needs. Long moments drag by before she returns her gaze to me.

"Baby?" she asks, miming her own stomach growing.

I smile and nod. She nods in return. I don't think it's a settled thing, but the idea has been presented. We have time if I get the epis for her. Which means getting to the city, dealing with the other, and somehow coming to terms. Surely, he needs my help too. Watching him help the humans, I'm certain he claimed at least one of them and the others are living in his territory without triggering his anger.

He has to be feeling responsible for them. It's my biggest hope for the two of us pushing past the bijass. If he's not too far gone.

Jolie speaks rapidly then points around. I point in the direction of the city. We're far off the path I had planned to take; skirting the edge of the territory I call my own. I don't come out this far very often but I'm familiar enough with it to get us where we need to go. The biggest concern will be others. When her ship crashed, there was such a bright light in the sky I know others will be traveling to investigate as well. I don't want to run into them on our journey. I have one to face at the end of my path and don't want to risk being weakened on the way. Thinking of that, my injured wing throbs reminding me that I'm already weak. Reaching over my shoulder, I massage the muscles trying to push blood into them and ease the discomfort.

Jolie watches, then speaks. She places her hand on mine, then walks behind me, inspecting the area. She says something that sounds sharp and harsh. Coming back in front, she speaks rapidly while moving her hands around in the air. She seems upset or maybe angry, but she's moving and talking so fast I can't follow what she's trying to communicate. She grabs the bag next to us and digs through it until she finds my jar of salve, unscrewing it as she walks behind me, and the next thing I know she's slathering my wing and the muscles on my back with it.

The salve goes on cool, then warms. My muscles unknot and the tension eases. When she walks back to the front, replacing the lid on the jar, she looks up at me and there is nothing but concern in her eyes. She places one hand back on my chest and asks a two-syllable word that ends as a question. I listen closely as she repeats it, then mimic it back to her.

"Ok?" she asks and I repeat it.

She points at my wing, then repeats the word. Smiling, I nod and cup her cheek in my hand. I give her a quick kiss then point, indicating we need to move. We have a long way to go and I want to get started. She puts the jar away, then we're off. Our journey is uneventful, if slow. I don't want to risk further damage to my wing until it's had time to heal, so I don't use them. This makes it easier to keep pace with Jolie's much slower speed, anyway. We trudge along through the sand, climbing dunes, and circumventing the rock formations. The closer we get the fewer formations of rock there are. The city sits on a vast plain. It was once one of the largest on the planet, called Drakonov in its prime, before the devastation.

The sun passes overhead. I make sure that Jolie drinks lots of water and chews on the dried guster meat. She slows as the day goes on, and her skin turns brighter and brighter shades of red. My concern for her grows. Then an idea occurs to me. I spread my wings, not to use them for running, but to create shade. I change positions so she's walking under the shadow of my uninjured wing. She smiles and perks up, the shade giving her at least some relief from the interminable heat.

As we climb the latest dune, this one the biggest yet, I hear something ahead of us. It's not an animal sound, there's something different about it. I listen as we walk then I realize it's the sound of metal on metal. Not a sound you hear out in the wilds of the planet. I stop walking and Jolie stumbles two steps ahead. I mime for her to crouch down. Through a series of complicated gestures that I repeat until I believe she understands I mean for her to stay. She tries to argue, but I hold up my hand and shake my head emphatically.

I go forward a few more feet until I'm close to the ridge, then lie down on the sand and vibrate myself back and forth until I'm camouflaged by the sand that covers me. Once done, I make my way to the ridge to see the source of the sound. A cold chill freezes my hearts. Zzlo.

The moment I see them I know what they are. Monsters from before the devastation. An entire race of slavers. The fear of them is inbred into all Zmaj. They starred in the tales used long ago to scare little children into being good. They have orange, leathery skin, and the tops of their heads are bald, ringed by black tentacles that hang down past their shoulders. Each tentacle is decorated with gold or silver bands that designate their rank within their own twisted society. They wear black leathers that a dim memory tells me are designed for survival in outer space.

There are six of them standing in a small group outside a ship. An entire, intact space ship. They're looking at machines in their hands and talking to each other. Spiked clubs hang on their hips, guns on the opposite, and swords are strapped to their backs. One of them is pointing off in the direction of my home but another pushes him against the chest and points towards the city. They're hunting. Damn it! They're here, and they're hunting.

There are too many of them for me to do anything about. They're better armed and outnumber me. I make my way back down the dune not taking my eyes off of them until the ridge blocks my view. Once I'm sure I'm out of their sight, I stand up from my camouflage then run to Jolie. She looks at me wide-eyed when I take her arm and pull her back down the dune. She starts to talk, but I cover her mouth with my hand and shake my head. She picks up on the seriousness of the situation, because she goes silent and does exactly what I want.

Once we're at the base of the dune, I get my bearings then plot a new course that will take us out and far around them. It will make our trip considerably longer but I can't risk running into them. I won't let them have her. I know the things they do to a girl like her.

Jolie moves close, inside my arms and leans her head against my chest while wrapping her arms around me. I put my arms around her too, and holding her tight I resolve that I will do whatever is needed to protect her. Nothing in this world will threaten her. She is mine. I will defend her against all comers including the monstrous Zzlo.

13

JOLIE

Something scared Sverre. I don't know what it is. He's being protective, which is nice, but worrisome at the same time. I want to know what could be so dangerous, so bad, that it could scare a Zmaj. On the other hand, maybe I don't want to know. We move on, but now there's a new urgency to his steps. Where before he was content to travel at my pace, now he's impatient with an intensity that's edged by fear. His eyes are never still. He scans the horizon without stopping. At any glint of the sun in the distance, any sound, his wings flutter and his hand drifts to his weapon.

He's nervous, and it's making me nervous too. The hairs on the back of my neck keep standing on end, and I'm doing my best to push past the exhaustion and pain of my body to make faster time. We walk in silence, too. Any time I speak, he places a finger against my lips and shakes his head, then looks around like he's making sure nothing is going to jump out of the sand and attack us.

We walk for what seems like forever, stopping each night and making camp. I lose track of how many days we spend in the sandy desert. Finally, one afternoon we clear a dune and

Ladon's city is in the distance. Skyscrapers jut into the red sky like broken teeth. The tops of most of them are sharp, broken angles. The sun glints off the remaining windows making the broken remains sparkle brightly in the distance.

No shields yet, damn it. I had a glimmer of hope that it might be running by the time I got back. I wonder if they've missed me. What am I thinking, of course they have! Oh, I wonder how big Calista is! How long have I been gone? Out in the wilderness with Sverre, days flowed by . Have they written me off for dead? Did they have a funeral for me? Oh! I can say some cool line, like if Calista says, "I thought you were dead," I'll reply with, "I was, but I'm better now." Yeah, that's a totally cool line! I know I saw that in more than one sci-fi show. We'll both get a laugh out of that one.

Everything's been so busy since Sverre took me away; I haven't really had time to realize how much I miss her. I can't wait to see her. Plus we now have something else in common! She has Ladon and I have Sverre. Which leads me to wonder, what do interspecies relationships do for double dating on a barren planet?

We pass out of the sand and into the city outskirts, but it's still a long way to get to the city center where Calista is probably going to be. Tall buildings with reflective glass line the streets. At one time, it was probably beautiful, but decay and neglect have taken a strong hold on the structures. Sverre seems to know his way around.

"Did you used to live here?" I ask just to break the oppressive silence.

Sverre stops walking and looks around before he looks at me. There's a sadness in his eyes and a heaviness in his manner. He doesn't try to say anything, just shakes his head and resumes walking.

It isn't long before we run into one of the work crews that are going from building to building looking for usable supplies. The humans are a quarter of a block ahead of us. One of them notices us and shouts something I can't make out. I wave as they stop in a huddle.

"Hey guys," I say once we're close enough I don't have to yell.

"What the hell are you doing with that?" an older, gray haired man says, pointing at Sverre.

"He's my friend, like Ladon," I reply.

There are four people in the work group. The one who spoke is the oldest, the other three are also men but younger. They stare at Sverre with their arms crossed. As we walk closer, they move into a tighter group and pull back a few steps.

"Just what we need, more aliens," Gray Hair says.

"Where's Rosalind?" I ask.

"Probably lording it over the city center like she usually is," one of the younger men mutters.

"Okay, well we should go," I say, pulling on Sverre's arm and walking past.

Sverre watches the men, turning his head to keep them in sight. Even once we're away, I can tell he's tense. His eyes are never still, he keeps me close to his side, and his wings rustle while his tail shifts from side to side in quick swipes. Maybe it's him, or it's the way those men acted. Something is off though. Nerves are making me feel on edge and, every time the wind rattles, I jump a little.

When we get close to the city center, Sverre slows. His agitation is now a palpable thing making the hair on my arms stand up. His hands clench repeatedly. A few people are out in the square doing something. Once we're close enough for me to spot Gershom, my heart sinks a little. Gershom was my boss back on the ship, head of the lab Calista and I worked in. He's also a super creep, though he had more of a thing for Calista than for me. Since we crashed, he's been an annoying pain in the ass. He's got a few of the survivors thinking like he does, they're all racist dicks.

The group looks over as we enter the city proper. It's a large, open square at the center of which is a pyramid-like structure. In front of the pyramid building is a block made of stone or concrete raised a foot from the ground that we've decided was once a fountain. In the middle of the fountain is a statue of Zmaj like Sverre or Ladon. The statue, twice as large as a real Zmaj, has its wings spread and holds a weapon similar to Sverre's at his side, while the other hand is raised towards the sky and holds long strands of something that looks like seaweed but I know now is epis.

It's all impressive to look at and takes my attention every time I see it. Which is probably why I miss the start of what happens next. I'm looking at the fountain, then trying to figure out what Gershom and the four men with him are doing, when something blurs, an impact sounds, and Sverre is no longer beside me. The air fills with roaring, and I'm lost in a confusion of fast motion coming quicker than I can process.

People are shouting. I whirl around trying to make sense of the blurring colors and the whirling blades. Something hits me, and I'm knocked back onto my ass where I sit stunned. Ladon is attacking Sverre! I can't believe my eyes but the two of them are engaged in what is obviously mortal combat. They both have their pole-arm sword weapons out and are spinning them rapidly around over their heads. With each spin, there is a thrust or a parry as they try to kill each other. They're roaring at each other in their own tongue.

"NO!" I scream. "LADON NO!"

Tears stream down my face as my throat is ripped raw with my scream. This can't be, this isn't the plan! We're going to double date; go see the colored dunes or something. This is all wrong! Neither of them pauses in their attacks, pressing against each other but it's only moments before I know that Sverre is giving ground to Ladon. My aching body has new bruises from my fall but I can't let this happen. I climb to my feet but I'm too slow.

Ladon swings his weapon in a circle over his head, then lashes out in an arc aimed at Sverre's neck. Sverre dodges, leaning to one side to avoid the blow that would have removed his head. The blade of the weapon grazes his arm, and in an unlucky break, catches between the scales, drawing first blood. He cries out in pain and my heart breaks.

"Sverre!" I scream, standing at last.

Sverre looks at me, but Ladon doesn't hesitate in his assault. He presses his advantage, driving Sverre further back. Sverre drops onto one knee underneath Ladon's swing, then comes up inside Ladon's reach. Sverre coughs, then a ball of fire erupts from his mouth, engulfing Ladon's face.

Ladon stumbles backwards screaming and swinging his weapon wildly. Sverre remains in a low crouch, creeping towards Ladon. I have to stop this. Ladon shakes his head from side to side, then stops. When he looks at Sverre, the rage is plain in his eyes. He throws down his weapon, spreads his wings and leaps up. He moves faster than Sverre can react, coming down with a raised fist that strikes Sverre across the face and sends him to the ground.

The sound of the impact is so loud it makes me hurt. Sverre lands on the ground with blood trickling from his mouth. Ladon is on top of him, beating him in a blind rage. Rushing forward, I grab Ladon's shoulder and try to pull him back, but he shrugs free and continues the beating.

"Ladon no!" Calista screams, arriving at last.

My hugely pregnant best friend runs out of the pyramid building straight to Ladon. She grabs his shoulder, so I grab the other side, trying to help. Ladon throws his head back and roars, his arms wide and his wings rustling while his tail swings wildly from side to side. He's shaking his head, but the sound of Calista's voice seems to calm him. He lets the two of us pull him back, neither of us big enough or strong enough to make him do anything he doesn't want to do. Calista holds his face in her hands and talks to him rapidly in his own tongue. She's the only human survivor lucky enough to have learned the language of the Zmaj. I kneel beside Sverre and my tears fall on his face.

"Are you okay? I'm so sorry! I had no idea that would happen. What the hell, Ladon?" I yell over my shoulder.

Calista is still talking to Ladon, and he's shaking. Physically shaking like he's struggling to control a rage that wants to consume him. His hands are clenched into fists, his jaw is a tight, hard line, and he's speaking in the harshest tone I've ever heard him use. Sverre stirs then moves into a sitting position. He grabs his jaw and moves it back and forth until it pops. I run my hands over him trying to determine if he has any wounds that need immediate attention. The cut on his arm is bleeding but not a lot and doesn't seem to be deep. He seems okay for the most part.

Sverre is watching Calista talk to Ladon, and it's easy to see he's shocked that she's speaking his language. He looks to me and I shrug, unable to explain. Ladon turns his back on Sverre and me as Calista pats his shoulder, then walks over to us.

"Hi," she says smiling.

Her belly is really starting to swell with her and Ladon's baby. She has a radiance about her, the glow of motherhood. Anger, fear, and relief war inside me and I can't move, stuck between my desire to throw my arms around her and my anger at what her boyfriend did to my lover. Tears stream down my face and Sverre puts a protective arm around my waist, pulling me close to his side.

Calista talks to Sverre in his language. Jealousy hits me so hard and fast it's enough to break through the warring emotions and take full precedence. He answers her and they talk back and forth. I wrap my hands around his arm and lean into him feeling protective. It's ridiculous, I know, but it doesn't change how I feel.

"Calista what in the hell is going on?" I ask as a growing crowd of survivors gathers to watch.

Half a dozen or so stand with Gershom and another half a dozen stand away from him. They're talking softly among themselves as latecomers are brought up to speed by those who witnessed it firsthand. My heart pounds in my chest. Looking at the gathering crowd, Ladon with his back to Sverre and me, Sverre sitting here hurt and talking with Calista—I don't know what to expect. None of this is the welcome home I thought I would receive. I've been gone, missing, and no one has asked if I'm okay. The man who saved me is attacked and brutally beaten as a thank you.

Calista continues speaking rapidly and Sverre answers her. Tightening my grip convulsively on Sverre's arm, rage builds inside me until I'm sure it's going to explode. A flash of white pushes through the crowd, then Rosalind arrives. Her long dark hair hangs past her shoulders and her uniform is still impeccably white. When she arrives anywhere, all eyes look to her. She takes control of a scene by her presence alone. The murmuring of the crowd silences under her gaze and even Ladon turns his attention to her. Calista stops talking to Sverre and turns towards Rosalind.

"Jolie," Rosalind says looking at me. "Are you okay?"

"Yeah," I say, unable to maintain my anger under the focus of her gaze.

"Good," she says. "We have a new arrival, I see."

The people with Gershom mutter but I can't make out the words, I can only say it doesn't sound friendly.

"This is Sverre," Calista says.

I glare at her as that stab of jealousy hits straight into my heart. He's mine, you've got yours! It's ridiculous, I know it, Calista is my best friend but I can't really help feeling this way with her able to talk to him while I can't without extreme gestures and mimicking.

"Welcome, Sverre," Rosalind says and holds her hand out to him.

Sverre stares at the hand then Calista says something, obviously explaining the gesture. Sverre takes the hand and shakes it but his eyes are still on Ladon.

"They were fighting!" Gershom yells. "We can't have that kind of violence in the city."

"I understand, Gershom," Rosalind says without so much as a glance in his direction. "Allow me to get a handle on the situation."

"Filthy animals," one of the men behind Gershom mutters, loud enough that everyone can hear it.

"They are not!" I scream, finding a focus for my pent up anger. Rosalind gives me a hard, cold look, pursing her lips. "They're not!" I insist. "Ladon attacked, unprovoked. Sverre didn't do anything."

I move protectively in front of Sverre. He places his large hand on my shoulder and says something, speaking soft, just to me. I turn to look at him and he shakes his head. Sadness resides in his eyes. He looks at Calista and speaks rapidly.

"What's he saying?" I ask her, but I can't take my eyes off of him.

An abyss is opening underneath my feet and I don't understand what's happening. It feels like everyone is in on some big joke and I'm the only one that doesn't know what's coming. Blood rushes to my cheeks, tears well in my eyes, and I'm shaking.

"He says it's a disease, they can't help it," Calista say both to me and Rosalind. "He had hoped they would be able to control it, rise above it, but it seems they can't."

"What are you talking about? He's nice! He saved me, he's protected me! It's crap." Tears fall as I try to deny what he's saying.

"Jolie," Calista says, her voice choking with unshed tears that shine in the corners of her eyes. "I know, I don't understand it all but he calls it bijass, it's a regression that the Zmaj are suffering from. Somehow, it makes them aggressive. It's why they don't live together. They can't, they can't resist it."

"No, this can't be. There has to be a way. I won't have it, he's mine. It's not fair," I cry turning to Rosalind.

"Fix this!" I yell at her. Calista moves towards me but I step back from her approach. "No, Ladon is your man. You get him under control. Somebody fix this. This can't be the way it is!"

Calista holds her hands up between us and the tears fall down her face now. "Jolie-"

"Don't you Jolie me! I've always stood by you, now I need you! You have to fix this. There has to be a way."

"We need time to understand," Calista says.

"No, no time. We can fix this. Damn it we're the smartest, the cleverest people on the planet. We can find an answer. We can fix this."

"Get the monster out of here," someone standing with Gershom says, but I can't see who through my tears.

"Piss off!" I scream. "He's not a monster."

Gershom steps up beside Rosalind. "Lady General," he says, his voice sweet and controlled.

"What, Gershom?" she asks.

"I would propose we banish the newcomer. We can't have this kind of violence erupting. The alien admits that they can't control their aggression. We have the one we know," he gestures at Ladon. "This one should go away, for the safety of our people."

Rosalind narrows her eyes and doesn't look at him. Her lips purse tight and it's plain to see she's considering it.

"No," I say my voice cracking. "No, you can't send him away."

"Until we understand this," Rosalind says. "It's for the best. He should leave the city, for now."

"NO!" I scream, turning and holding on to Sverre.

His turquoise eyes stare into mine with sadness and he reaches up to wipe a tear from my cheek. Calista is speaking and he may be listening to her too, but his attention is on me. He leans in and kisses me, his strong arms wrapping around my waist. Then he lets me go. He says something, then hands are on me, pulling me away from him. I fight against them, struggling for all I'm worth. Screaming his name, clawing at the people holding me back.

Sverre talks to Calista, then he locks eyes with me. He shakes his head and I stop struggling. Once I do, he nods, then he turns and heads out of the city. As I watch him walk away, my heart shatters as everything I've ever wanted falls to pieces. I collapse into my tears and Calista gathers me into her arms. Sobs shake my body as I cling to her.

"It's okay, I'll fix this," she whispers, running her hands along my hair. "Somehow."

Her words are meaningless to me. I've never felt this empty before.

14

SVERRE

I should have known better. Ladon is too far gone to the bijass. I couldn't get him to listen to reason no matter how I tried. When he drew blood, I lost control too. Damn it! The look on Jolie's face as I walked away is seared into my memory. I don't think I've ever had to make a harder choice but the one who claims to be her friend, Calista, made sense.

We won't overcome the bijass by brute force. I have to be smarter than that. I should have made my presence known before entering the heart of Ladon's territory. Met him on neutral ground somewhere. If I hadn't been distracted by the Zzlo, I would have thought of it, but I was driven by dimly-remembered fears and my need for help to save Jolie. Now I've messed things up, again.

Sitting on a dune looking down at the city below me, I chew on a piece of dried bivo meat and contemplate what to do now. I'm not leaving Jolie, not for long. When I told Calista what Jolie had been through, she promised they could help her. I told Calista that Jolie needed epis and she understood. How does that one know my language while Jolie does not? It's not fair. I want to talk with Jolie and understand every word. I want to know her thoughts, her feelings, I want to hear her musical voice and have it form pictures in my mind.

Damn it. How long before the Zzlo find the city? Jolie's people are not ready for an attack. None of the city defenses are activated, and the people there didn't appear to have any weapons to speak of. Ladon alone won't be able to stand against a Zzlo assault. We have to get past the bijass. It's more important than ever with the slavers here. I wanted it at first for Jolie but now it's a matter of both our races surviving.

The sun is dropping behind the city illuminating it with its last rays. The buildings light up outlined in fiery red. It's beautiful but stirs old, unwanted memories of pain so I push them back into the mists. She will come soon. She promised. If she really is Jolie's friend, she will show up. If not then I will invade his territory again but this time I won't come in peace. Jolie is mine and I won't let them keep me from her for long, no matter what it takes.

Shadows creep over the striated sand dunes, chasing away the final beams of light. I scavenge for material to start a fire. As darkness reclaims the land, I find enough for my purposes. I breathe onto the small pile of debris, letting out fire from the glands in the back of my throat, and the kindling catches. I feed some of the bigger pieces slowly into the fire, but not too many. I don't want anything that attracts too much attention, just enough to guide Calista to my position as we agreed.

Once the fire is self-sufficient, I settle back and wait. I try to focus on nothing, to clear my mind of all thoughts, emotions, and distractions, but it's impossible. The look on Jolie's face as I walked away rises unbidden. The pain in my chest, the irregular rhythm of my hearts returns, making it feel like a massive hand is crushing my chest. My eyes fly open and all focus is gone. The memory of Jolie's anguish is pulling me back to the now, back to my pain.

A shadow darts out of the city below.

I move back from the fire then crouch in the shadows outside its ring of light. The figure heads right for the fire, making a beeline. I wait.

Calista steps into the ring of light and looks around. She's a pretty enough girl, though no comparison to Jolie. Though it's obvious they are of the same species, there are many differences between them. Jolie is tiny and has a golden tint to her skin when she's not being burned by the harsh sun. Calista is paler and her eyes are shaped differently. Her nose is bigger as well and there is the swell of her stomach. I wonder if she's pregnant. If she is, and she's with Ladon, which she claims, is it his baby? She looks around, not spotting me at first. I've noticed that Jolie's night vision is poor as well.

"Hello," Calista says as I step into the ring of light.

"Greetings," I say keeping the distance between us. "How is Jolie?"

"Upset," she answers honestly, which I appreciate. "But she understands, and is on board with my plan."

"Good," I say, holding back my thoughts of what I will do if I discover she is not telling me the truth. Threats are petty and unnecessary.

"Can you explain this... bijass... to me?" She stumbles over the word but gets the pronunciation right.

I motion for her to take a seat, then do the same, moving closer to the fire so we can see each other clearly. I offer her some of my dried meat, which she politely refuses. The needs of hospitality met, I now feel I can talk to her in earnest.

"It's in our genetics," I say. "You are familiar with this concept? The way creatures are made up?"

"Yes, Jolie and I are both scientists. We study plants and the evolution of life."

"Good," I say smiling. I knew my Jolie was smart but hearing Calista say it fills me with pride. "Ladon may not be familiar with it. He is a warrior, and this was hidden from our people. No one wants to know where you come from, what you are made of, so we kept it hidden."

"How do you know he's a warrior?" she asks, resting her hands on her swollen belly.

"His markings, his build, it's obvious."

"I'm sorry for interrupting, please continue," she says.

"First, how is it you speak my language?" I ask. "You're fluent in it. Why can Jolie not speak it?"

She smiles and looks down at her stomach, rubbing her hands along it. "There's a machine in the pyramid building that we call City Hall," she says. "I accidentally got it to work, but haven't been able to figure out how to do it again. Somehow, it taught me your language. I don't understand it. It's not a technology my people have, but I've been trying to figure it out."

I cast my mind back, and memory of the machine returns. "I think I can activate it—I remember it from before. You know of the devastation?"

"Yes, I've seen videos from before, though I don't understand all of it. You can activate the machine?"

I nod, but that line of thought is leading me into the fog of memories I don't want to deal with right now, so I change direction.

"The bijass," I say, redirecting the conversation. "It's a genetic flaw that has only come to the fore because of the devastation. After it was over, those of us who survived found each other. I don't remember how or why, but we separated. It was the choice we made at the time. I'm sure it seemed wise, but it exacerbated the flaw. The more time we spend alone, the more primal we become. It's a regression. It's subtle and you don't even realize it's happening to you. Territory comes first. After that, it's a fight for survival over resources, the necessary things to live. It seems reasonable to keep others out of what you claim for your own. Then you start collecting treasures. Things that are useful, at first, but that grows too, and you collect things that have value only to you. Memories fade. That's the curse and the bliss of it. The further the bijass takes hold of you, the more a sort of fog covers over the past."

"That sounds awful," she says, sadness heavy in her voice.

"No, it's perfect," I stare into her eyes.

"Why?" she asks.

"Memories are pain. We're a doomed race. Do you want to be reminded of that every day of your very long life?"

She shakes her head and moisture falls down her cheek just like Jolie. The comparison returns the throbbing ache in my chest, the ache of missing her, though I have only been without her for a few hours.

"I understand," she says. "Is that why you and Ladon fought?"

"Yes," I say.

"I heard you arguing with him as I ran up."

"Yes, I was trying to get him to see reason. To break him free of the grip of the bijass," I say.

"So it's possible?" she asks.

"I believe so," I say. "I was able to resist it until he drew blood. Then I lost control, to my shame."

She nods, biting her lower lip. "Okay, let me talk to him. Maybe if he knows you're coming, that would help. We could find some way to create a gradient, let him fight it a piece at a time."

I nod my agreement. "There's something more, something that might, if he remembers, help."

"What is it?" she asks.

"Zzlo," I say.

"What's that?"

"Slavers. They're here, not far away. A lot of them, too many for even a mighty warrior like Ladon to take alone."

"Slavers? What do they look like?"

As I describe them she turns pale, then one hand covers her mouth as she gasps.

"You know them?" I ask.

"They were the monsters that attacked our ship, they caused us to crash. There's more of them here? We found some remains of a crashed ship. I thought they'd died."

"These didn't crash. Their ship is intact."

"Damn," she says.

"I agree. Tell Ladon; make him understand that we have to join forces. He should know there will be others coming too."

"Others?"

"Yes, other Zmaj. When your ship came down, there was a huge blast in the sky. I'm sure at least half the planet could see it. My territory is close to his so I arrived first, but don't make the mistake of thinking I'm the only one coming. There will be others."

She frowns. We sit in silence while she thinks and I wait.

"Okay," she says at last.

She struggles to rise to her feet, her swollen belly throwing her off balance. I help her then step back.

"May I ask a question?"

"Of course," she says.

"Are you pregnant?"

She smiles gently, then laughs. "Yeah, I'm not just fat."

"Ah," I reply, debating whether I have the right to ask my next question.

She steps closer to me and places a hand on my chest, just

like Jolie does. We stare into each other's eyes and I feel like she's searching for something. I meet her gaze and wait, letting her decide for herself if she finds what she's looking for.

"You love her?" she asks at last.

I don't answer immediately. I think about that. Is that what this is? It's been so long since I've felt any emotions other than the bijass-driven need for treasure.

"I think so," I say at last. I can love as a man—I am not lost to the monster.

"Good," Calista says and steps back, removing her hand from my chest. "She needs love. She deserves it. But I'll tell you right now, if you ever hurt her I'll have Ladon kick your ass again."

I couldn't stop my smile if I wanted to. The fierceness of Calista warms my heart. I see clearly that she is Jolie's friend, and worthy of the name.

"Understood," I say. "Can you make it back on your own?"

"Yeah, no problem. I'll handle Ladon. Give me a couple of days okay? Then I'll come back and get you, once it's all worked out."

"Tell Jolie I'm close, please?" I ask of her.

She smiles and disappears into the darkness outside the fire. I watch her shadowy figure as she darts back to the city, then sit down to wait.

15

JOLIE

I don't know where Calista is. Rosalind had me taken to a room in City Hall and asked that I wait. She may have asked, but the fact that there are two men standing outside the door makes it clear it was a hell of a lot more than a request. I can't believe how wrong everything has gone. They kicked Sverre out of the city and he left, leaving me behind. I know he didn't want to. I could see in his eyes it was tearing him apart.

And now I'm alone. Calista came by, told me she was trying to work things out, but it's obvious that things are changing. The people who run with Gershom are grumbling and causing problems. It hasn't taken long for petty human politics to rear its ugly head. I guess we should be thankful it waited until our survival wasn't so much in question.

How do I fix this?

I pace the room. It's twenty feet across. I've counted every step trying to clear my head. The door handle turns and when it opens, I expect to see Calista. Instead, Gershom walks in. My stomach roils with acid at the sight of him. He takes a seat, uninvited, then motions that I should sit down as well. I stand just to spite him.

"What the hell is this?" I ask.

"I thought maybe we should have a talk," Gershom says.

"I'm not interested," I say.

"Fine. I'll talk, you listen. Many of us are concerned about this new... creature you brought uninvited into our home."

"One, he's not a creature, he's a man. Two, it was his home first, so what the hell are you going on about?"

Anger flashes in Gershom's eyes as his right hand clenches into a fist. "He's not a man," he says through tight lips.

"More of a man than you," I say.

Gershom doesn't respond. He sits watching me and the tension between us builds.

"He's not your kind," he says at last.

"Not my kind how?" I ask.

"He's not human."

"No? Really? What was your first clue? The wings or the tail?"

"Are you really so blind? Our survival depends on us banding together!" Gershom growls.

"In what, some kind of stand for racial purity? What does it matter to you? It's none of your business."

"Our women need to be ours. Do you realize how few of us there are left? We've got one abomination happening already. Are we to stand by and let these animals take our women?"

I stare at him in disbelief. He said that. I can't believe it but he literally said those words. I slap his face with every-thing I've got. It happens before I even think about it. The imprint of my hand is red on his face.

"Animals! You're an animal. You're such a, ugh! Asshole!" I

scream, unable to form my thoughts into words past my disbelief and anger.

"I hoped you'd see reason," he says, rubbing his cheek as he stands. "I see I was mistaken."

He walks to the door and opens it so I grab the chair he was sitting in and throw it at him. He must hear what I'm doing because he dodges and the chair slams against the wall with a bang.

"There's your 'reason,'" you xenophobic son of a bitch!"

He rushes out the door. How many of them are there? How many of my fellow humans agree with what he just said? Screw this; I'm not staying here any longer. I'll go to Sverre and we'll leave. I don't need this kind of attitude or thinking.

When I open the door, the two men standing to either side turn and look at me. They're not armed but they look threatening. Screw it, they can't stop me. I storm between the two of them.

"You're supposed to stay here," one of them says.

"Says who?" I ask, whirling on the speaker.

"Lady General Rosalind," he says, taking a step back from my wrath.

"Are you with him?" I scream as I stalk towards him waving a finger in his face. "You believe his bullshit?"

The man's eyes widen, his mouth falls open and he back steps. "I don't know what you're talking about," he says.

"What about you?" I ask the other, putting my finger in his face.

"Hey, just doing what the Lady asked," he says, holding his hands up palms facing me. "Innocent here."

"Good, good to both of you. If Rosalind wants me I'm going to my bunk."

"Are you sure?" the first speaker asks.

"Why wouldn't I be sure?" I ask.

"Because there is more going on than you know about," Rosalind says from behind me.

My anger is gone in an instant, sapped away by Rosalind's calm and in control voice. My shoulders slump as I turn to face her. She's taller than me, as is most of the world, so I have to look up to her, but there's something about her that makes everyone feel like they have to look up to her.

"What is it?" I ask. "What is going on around here? Has everyone gone insane?"

"Maybe," she says. "Let's go back in the room where we can talk more privately."

If it was anyone but Rosalind, I would argue but I can't, not with her. It doesn't even occur to me until I'm walking through the door I just stormed out of, that maybe I should. Rosalind picks up the chair I threw, rights it, then places it and sits down. I sit opposite her.

"What's going on, Rosalind?" I ask. "I wasn't gone that long. What the hell changed?"

She eyes me for a long moment looking thoughtful before she answers. "Do you know how many survivors there are?"

"Um, a couple of hundred?" I guess.

"Just over three hundred."

"Okay, so that's more than I thought."

"Do you know how many of the survivors are women?"

"No," I say.

"Thirty-two percent," she replies grimly. Then it clicks home for me.

This is where Gershom is gathering his power. He's playing into the men's fears of being alone forever. A fear I know, because I was feeling it too.

"So three guys for every girl. Do they all think like Gershom?" I ask.

"No, but he is gathering...like-minded individuals."

"Shit," I say and Rosalind nods as I think through the

implications. "So Calista, who Gershom wanted anyway, chooses an alien, and then I come home with one too, shit."

"Exactly," Rosalind says.

"It's not right though. You can't choose who you love! That's not how it works. I mean the heart wants what the heart wants right?"

"Do you love him?" she asks.

"I—" I cut myself off. Do I? Is that what I'm saying?

That takes things to a whole new level. Love? I can't even talk to him really. Then I think about what we've been through. The way he treats me. I said I wanted a man who looked at me like Ladon looks at Calista. Sverre does that, and so much more. He's gruff and grumpy outside but with me he's gentle and kind and oh so thoughtful. He makes me feel safe...wanted...valued. Is that love? It's part of it.

He's strong and sexy as hell. I like his quiet thoughtfulness, and he's willing to risk everything for me. He almost died to save me when I fell into that hole. He came to the city, and I have no doubt he knew that Ladon would try to hurt him, but he did it for me.

Rosalind watches me in silence, letting me work it out for myself. When I walked out of this room, before she came, I was going to gather my things and leave to find him. Is that love?

"I don't honestly know."

She sighs. "Then here we are," she says. "Calista has been to talk with Sverre. She is with Ladon now convincing him to let Sverre into the city."

"What about Gershom and the others who think like him?" I ask.

"We'll cross that bridge when we have to."

Leaning back in my chair, I think about what she's told me. A few hundred of us. There were so many more on the ship.

"Do you think there are more?" I ask.

"More what?" she replies.

"Survivors," I say.

"It is possible," she says, thoughtful. "I've considered it. The colony ship was massive and only one part was in sight of where we crashed. It's possible that other parts of it crashed in completely different areas of the planet, depending on how they hit the atmosphere."

"We should find them!"

Rosalind gives me a look that makes it very clear she's already thought of that.

"When we're ready," she says.

"Ready for what?"

"To survive," she says simply. "We're barely able to feed the ones who are already here. Water is in short supply, and epis is extremely difficult to get. We can't take on more survivors."

I nod understanding. "I get it."

"Good," she says as the door opens and Calista walks in.

Calista comes straight to me and grabs me up into a tight embrace. Her tears wet my shoulder as she grips me. I hug her tightly. Her swelling belly forces me to bend at the waist, and I swear I feel it kicking. Calista lets me go but holds on to my shoulders.

"Don't you EVER do that again!" she yells at me.

"What?" I'm surprised to be yelled at when she was just hugging me.

Calista wipes the tears from her face. "I was so scared. I thought you were dead when we couldn't find you after the second day. I can't do this," she motions to her belly, "alone. Don't you dare try to leave me."

"Okay, I won't," I say.

"Are you okay?"

"Yeah, I'm fine. Dehydrated but I'm good. How's Ladon?" I ask.

"He's having a difficult time, but he's working on it," Calista says. "And your man, Sverre, is fine too."

"You've spoken to him?" I ask, unable to keep my voice from cracking with excitement.

"Yeah," she says.

"When did you speak to him?" Rosalind interrupts, rising to her feet.

"Uh, about three hours ago," Calista says, avoiding her glare.

"I said no one was to leave the city after dark," Rosalind says.

"I know. I had to work this out. Gah, there's so much I need to tell you but I should tell everyone at once," Calista says.

"Everyone?" I ask, wondering who is included in that.

"We've formed a Council in your absence," Rosalind says.

"Oh, okay. So is Ladon going to let Sverre back in?"

"Yes," Calista says and relief floods through me.

"Good. What the hell was that? Why did he attack Sverre?"

"That's part of what I need to brief everyone about. And there are new threats looming. Right now though, Ladon's agreed to keep his temper in check. We'll just need to be careful. I'll explain more while we walk. We need to go get Sverre then get the Council together."

"We can go get him? Now?" I ask, bouncing on the balls of my feet.

"Yes," Calista says, then pauses and looks at Rosalind. "With your permission Lady General."

"Why not? I need all the able bodies I can get my hands on."

16

SVERRE

*M*y chest aches with a pulsing emptiness that is aggravated by every breath I take. Every beat of my hearts is a reminder of what I've left behind. What I've done. I left her. My primal instincts berate me for not fighting Ladon to the end. For not destroying him rather than leaving Jolie behind. I can't push her face out of my memory. The water falling from her eyes as I walked away.

I walked away. I did. I left her.

But it was the right move, my better self insists. I'm on my feet and walking back to the city before I even realize it, but I stop myself. I told Calista I would give her time to work this out, and I'm a man of my word. A man, not the beast the bijass would make me.

Hours pass while my thoughts fight round after round with the bijass. I wait. Patience has never been a trait I've possessed. The sun sets and still I think of her. Reason wars with desire for action, but reason continues to win. I feed my tiny campfire; just enough for a signal light really, and stare at the city. At last, I see motion at the edge. One shadow crosses from civilization to the encroaching sand, then three more follow it. The fact that so many are coming sets off blaring alarms in my mind. I expected Jolie and maybe one more. Is this a group coming to kill me? Have they harmed Jolie?

Rage grips my thoughts and a plan forms. I move outside the ring of light cast by my small fire, then lie flat. I wriggle and vibrate until I am hidden in the cooler layer under the surface of the sand. My hearts beat out of time pushing adrenaline into my system. Tension builds, muscles quiver in readiness. I'll destroy them all if they've hurt her. Reason urges caution, fighting against the rage as I wait. I see them climbing the dunes but it's too dark to make out who approaches. One of them is large and I'm certain it's Ladon. The others are shorter and smaller. One is short enough to be Jolie. Is it her? My hearts increase their speed. My limbs vibrate with pent up energy, ready to leap to her rescue.

The figures slow their approach. I hear them talking, unsure why the circle of light is empty. The smallest one motions to the others and then steps forward. When the figure reaches the edge of the light, I see it's her. Jolie! She appears unharmed but I hesitate. Is she trying to signal me? Warn me of danger?

"Sverre?" she asks, her musical voice soft. She turns in a circle. "Are you here?"

I leap from hiding, crossing the distance between us in two strides with my wings spread. I maneuver her behind me in a single motion, facing the others with my lochaber at the ready.

"Who comes?" I challenge.

A woman in white steps forward with her hands held up and to either side with palms facing me. She speaks in her own tongue and Calista translates.

"We're friends, Sverre," Calista says. "Ladon came so you know that you're welcome. He understands."

Ladon steps forward and lowers his hood. He holds out his arms, palms up, fingers pointing at me in a gesture of peace. Staring into one another's eyes, neither of us speaks. No one moves, all eyes are on Ladon and me. Sheathing my lochaber, I cross the distance between us and lay my hands down on his.

"Headman," Ladon says.

"Warrior," I say, also acknowledging who he was and is.

Ladon nods then steps back.

"Come, be welcome in my territory. No harm shall come to you while you are under my care," Ladon says.

"I accept your welcome. I bring only friendship and good will into your home," I respond to his formality.

The tension is gone. Jolie places a hand on the small of my back above my tail. She stands beside me. I turn to her with a smile that I can't hide. She rises up on her toes and I lean in to meet her. We kiss, softly and longingly. Rosalind clears her throat.

"We should really get back, there's a lot to do," she says, interrupting our kiss.

Reluctant though I am, I agree with her assessment. They take us into the city with Ladon in the lead. We don't see any others as we travel. When we reach the town center, the group moves into the Hall of Leadership.

"We've arranged sleeping quarters for Jolie and you," Calista says while Ladon stands by silently. "In the morning we'll meet and discuss what's next. Now we should all sleep."

Calista looks between Jolie and me with a smile that makes it clear she doesn't expect us to do much sleeping. I smile too, feeling my arousal stir. Calista says something in her own language to Jolie, who nods and then takes my hand and leads us away from the others. Deep into the building we go, moving quickly. No words are necessary. The desire between us is all the communication either of us needs.

Before the door to our room is even closed behind us, she's in my arms, our lips smashing together with bruising force. She leaps and wraps her legs around my waist. My prime penis is instantly hard and ready for her. Holding her against me, I stagger across the room, bumping into the furniture in my passionate haste. Finally, we crash into a couch and tumble across it.

Passion burns hot. My hands wander across the cloth she wears, desperate to touch her skin. I need to feel her close to me, taste all of her. I want to know every part of her intimately. She's so delicate, such a beautiful treasure. All my fears of losing her, of someone harming her, stoke the fire of my desire.

Her hands lock behind my neck. Kissing along her cheek, I cross down her neck and along her shoulder. My hands roam around her hips, up her sides, and then find her breasts. So soft and unprotected. So enticing.

Gripping her shirt at the top, I rip it aside with no patience for the fastenings. The protective, stretchy cloth covers them but I pull it down revealing the dark centers of her soft mounds. I take one in my mouth, circling its point with my tongue.

"Sverre," she moans, pushing forward.

I stroke her beautiful body, delighting in the feel of her skin. I fumble with the fastener of her pants, trying to open them while continuing my attention on her soft breast.

Her hand touches mine then moves it aside, and she undoes her pants for me. She lifts her hips and I slide them down, taking the cloth underneath at the same time. The scent of her fills my senses and my cock rages with need, demanding to be buried in her.

I leave a trail of kisses across her flat stomach and kiss my way to her leg, dragging my tongue across her skin. Bumps rise on her flesh as I taste down her leg to her knee then up the inside of her thigh. I pause to nibble her delicate skin. The scent of her fills my nostrils, calling to me, pulling me in, increasing my desire. My cock throbs, begging for her, but I won't give in yet.

She shivers as I close with the fur that covers her mound. I lick the fold between her leg and center before I move up and then across, just above her sweet opening then I pass down to her other leg. I nibble my way down to her knee. She shivers and shakes, then locks her hands behind my head, tugging me towards her. But I won't be hurried. My tongue wants to taste her sweetness; my cock wants to be buried in her. I won't give in to desire before I'm ready. I paint a line on her leg with my kisses, making her shiver with each one.

Reaching her soft center, I lick her opening carefully, not penetrating her silky folds. She pulls hard trying to bring me closer but I resist. When I reach the top of her opening, I tease the folds until my tongue just broaches her outer lips. I lick up her sweetness, and the taste of her on my tongue almost makes me lose control. Desire roars, my cock jumps, and I want to drive in. Still, I resist though it's become harder as I'm almost blinded by my desire and need for her. I continue licking slowly, working my way deeper until her innermost folds open themselves to me. A delicate nub appears, coming out to meet my seeking tongue. I push my tongue deeper inside her then drag up and down. The nub glistens and grows, demanding attention.

"Sverre!" she exclaims as she uses her hands behind my head to force me hard against her.

I let her pull me in and I hold my rough tongue flat against the exposed nub that causes such a reaction in her. She bucks against me, so I hook my arms under her legs and grab her hips. I pull her tight, forcing myself hard against her sweet taste and moving my head slowly sideways then up and down. I lift up and my tongue is deep inside her, teasing her until she cries out. Her muscles stiffen and she locks her legs around my head.

As her muscles unclench and her legs relax, I lower her back to the couch. I slowly pull back from her mound, letting her relax. She spreads her legs and I rise until my cock is at her entrance, ready and full of need. She smiles at me with half-lidded eyes, heavy with pleasure and desire.

"Sverre," she moans.

I push forward slowly and find that she's wet, so much so that it feels amazing. I never knew how good wetness could feel. The tip of my cock rests inside her wetness and it's incredible.

We lie together, neither of us moving, as we enjoy the sensation of coming together. I wait until the pulsing need of my core won't let me wait any longer, then I push in.

Her body responds, expanding to accommodate. I give it time to adjust to my girth and size. One ridge then the next slides in and she moans. Her body closes around my cock as each bit penetrates. It takes all my will not to drive in. I continue going slowly until I'm fully buried.

Wetness pours from her down my shaft, pulling me in deeper, welcoming me. I slide out, slow, keeping it easy, then sliding faster. She thrusts her hips against me and rotates them in a circle when I'm fully inserted, and then we retreat.

We pull back and forth, building. My testicles tighten as my pleasure grows. My prime penis spasms as I piston deep. I can't hold back for long.

"Sverre!" she cries out, throwing her arms back over her head and thrusting forward.

I spill my seed into her, pumping it out fast and hard. My cock spasms, jumping as I come.

We kiss. I pull my soft cock out and the second rises, ready. My desire is still hot. She breaks our kiss and smiles, then pushes me back. As I lean away, she rolls over to rest her top half on the back of the couch while her beautiful hind side is up in the air.

I let my hand roam across the soft globes, spreading the crack open to reveal her pink holes. She's beautiful everywhere. My cock throbs with my want and need. I close with her and pause as my cock is pressing against her opening once more.

Sliding in is like entering heaven. Every sense is overwhelmed, thought is consumed. The wetness, the way her body closes on my cock, the throbbing of her slick tunnel as I slide deeper in. She moans and I softly hiss her name.

"Jj-oo-leeee."

Her grip tightens on the back of the couch as I push in to the hilt. Grabbing her hips, I hold her tight against me while rocking just slightly back and forth. She hangs her head down and pants some word over and over.

I begin moving in and out and she pushes back into me with each thrust forward. She's so tight my tipping point is already close. I can barely contain myself. With each thrust, she moans beautifully. Her voice is like magic, calling to me, coaxing my pleasure.

My cock stiffens and I'm almost there. I won't be able to hold out much longer. Grabbing her hips, I pull her tight against me and hold. My cock spasms and I lose my self-control.

She cries out. Her back arches and her toes curl as she moans. I pull out of her and we collapse into each other's arms.

We kiss and she snuggles up against me with her head on my shoulder. I smile as she falls asleep within moments.

17

JOLIE

*S*leeping next to Sverre makes me happy. I wake up feeling refreshed. I'm still achy and dry as can be but that's to be expected.

Sverre is awake before me. When I roll over, he smiles and pulls me even closer with one arm. He leans in and we kiss.

"Good morning," I say, not caring that he still can't understand me.

We get up together and dress. Calista really is the best friend a girl could ask for. She set this room up for us ahead of time knowing that I'd want to be alone with him. No matter what else, I love the way he makes me feel.

Sverre says something and I shake my head. Closing with me, he touches my lips then my throat. He then motions towards himself and repeats the gesture.

"I don't understand," I say.

He frowns and tries again but I can't figure out what he's trying to tell me. He gives up and walks to the door so I follow along. He moves through the building with confidence. It's obvious he knows his way around. It's not a big leap of logic to guess that he's been here before, and I'd guess often, with the certainty he's displaying. The direction he's leading will take us to the labs that Calista and I have been using to study the plant life and experiment on getting our supply of earth seeds to grow in this soil.

Before we get that far he turns into a room with glass cubicles. This room Calista discovered when Ladon first brought her to the city. She says it's where she learned Ladon's language but no one has been able to figure it out since. Sverre walks up to a cubicle and begins tapping at the input device. He works for a few minutes and the screen in front of him flashes with different colors and symbols. The machine flashes yellow and he hisses.

He turns around, obviously angry, so I stand back, letting him work. He goes from terminal to terminal repeating the same actions, as far as I can tell. When he reaches the last one, he hisses again, then opens up his bag and digs through it. He pulls out a wooden box. I recognize it from his home. I hadn't realized he'd brought it along with him. He holds it in both hands staring at it with what looks like reverence, or maybe disgust. It's such an odd mix of emotions playing across his face.

He opens the box and stares at the shield inside. Shaking his head, he takes it out of the box, places it in the palm of his hand, then presses it against the input board. The screen flashes yellow then blue then green and symbols stream across it. He says something that ends in a long hiss. He looks over at me and motions for me to come closer. Walking over, my heart rate increases, knowing something is about to happen.

Gently he takes me by my shoulders and positions me in front of the machine. He steps to one side then reaches in and taps the input device. A white light flashes into my eyes and everything spins. I'm ripped apart into a million pieces strewn across the universe. I blink and I'm standing in a field of white that goes for as far as my eyes can see. It flows into me. As I pull back together and return to self-awareness, I know. As if I've known it all my life, something I learned as a child.

I stumble backwards, blink rapidly, and the white field is gone. Colors dance before my eyes but clear as I continue blinking. My breath is coming in ragged gasps. Nausea passes over me in a wave that causes me to double over. Sverre is holding me up so I brace myself against him.

"Thank you," I say.

"You're welcome," he says and I know it.

The entire world stops as I look into his eyes. I understood him and he understood me. He keeps an arm wrapped around me until I'm steady.

"Sverre," I say and his name rolls off my tongue easier. I don't have to concentrate on it like I did before to make sure I get the sounds right. He smiles. "Sverre!"

As I take his hands in mine, a wave of euphoria passes through me. We can talk! My heart expands and my chest feels like I'm filling with more air than I can hold. I could float away I'm so ecstatic. I can't think of any words to say so I throw my arms around him.

"There you two are," Calista says behind me. When I turn around I have tears in my eyes and she stops as I try to wipe them away. "Are you okay?"

"She is fine," Sverre answers before I can. "I've fixed the machine. It should work for anyone now."

My throat is choked up with emotions too strong to be contained. I nod and wipe at the tears until the lump in my throat finally clears enough so I can talk.

"That's great!" Calista says. "I'll get the others down here. Can you show me how to run it?"

I notice that Sverre keeps the badge palmed in his hand but I don't say anything.

"Yes," he says, turning his back to Calista and me and reaching into his pack. When he turns around the box and the badge are gone. I'll have to ask him about that later, but I can tell that he doesn't want attention called to it right now. Sverre shows Calista and me how to run the machine. It's simple now that he's unlocked it.

In the next hour, we find our friends and they all agree to learn the language. Rosalind, Amara, Inga, Lana, and Mei all use the machine. As Mei finishes, Rosalind looks the group over.

"We should ask Gershom if he'd like to," she says.

"Why? He's a dick," Amara says, speaking the thought that's on all our minds.

"Peace," Rosalind says. "We can't afford internal strife. We are too few and too dependent on each other. He is part of the Council."

"Yeah, but he's a douche," Amara continues to hold out. "I mean like, epic-level super-douche. He's like the Lich King of Douchebaggery."

I snort.

"She's right," Calista agrees.

"Be that as it may," Rosalind says, taking the high road. "He has a seat on the Council. The offer should be extended. It might help ease the interspecies tension as well."

"I doubt it. Once a douche, always a douche, but whatever," Amara says.

"I'll go find him," Mei says, and runs off.

We make small talk and everyone wants to hog Sverre's attention now that they can speak to him freely. It's not long before Mei returns with Gershom, and three other men are with him. None of them look happy.

"Gershom," Rosalind greets him. "The machine is working. You can learn the Zmaj language, which will aid us in working together for our mutual survival."

"Our mutual survival?" Gershom asks, looking us over like we're insects.

The three men with him stand with their arms crossed, glaring.

"Yes," Rosalind says simply.

"Our mutual survival is not my concern, Lady General," Gershom says. "Survival of our race is. I won't learn their language. We don't need them for our survival. We need to support our own race."

"Fine," Rosalind says unperturbed. "The Council is convening now."

She walks past Gershom who almost is bold enough to stand in her way, only moving at the last possible moment. We follow Rosalind upstairs and she leads us to a room with double doors. On the other side of it is a large table with chairs. She takes a seat at the head and Gershom sits beside her. The rest of us choose seats and Sverre sits next to me, we hold hands underneath the table.

"Where's Ladon?" Rosalind asks.

"I think he's on his way," Calista says.

"Fine, we'll wait," Rosalind says.

"No, we need to start now." Gershom intrudes. "I've been thinking, we should send patrols out to see if other pieces of the colony ship landed with survivors as well."

"Gershom," Rosalind says, her voice quiet. "I said we'll wait."

"And I said we'll begin, we are, after all, co-chairs of this council."

The two of them glare at each other, but the point becomes moot when the door opens and Ladon walks in. He stares at Sverre for a long moment that makes the hair on back of my neck stand on end. Tearing his gaze away, he walks over and takes his seat next to Calista.

"The Council is convened," Rosalind says, repeating herself in both languages. I notice Gershom rolls his eyes.

"Welcome our guest," Rosalind says, nodding to Sverre. "He has things to report to us."

Sverre stands, placing both hands on the table in front of him. He clears his throat before speaking.

"Greetings," he says. "Thank you to the mighty warrior Ladon for allowing me to enter his territory."

Rosalind translates for Gershom, no one else cares enough that he understands.

Ladon nods in response and holds his hands up over the table with his palms facing the ceiling. Sverre places his hands in front of himself with palms down. Both men put their hands down.

"There are threats that you may not be aware of," Sverre says, his eyes on Ladon. "Zzlo have landed on the planet."

"NO!" Ladon says jumping to his feet, anger rolling off of him in waves.

Everyone is on their feet. Ladon is shaking with anger. Sverre stands stock still staring at Ladon.

"Wait!" I yell to be heard over the cacophony of everyone talking at once.

Everyone looks at me. Ladon sits down staring at Sverre.

"You're wrong," Ladon says.

"What the hell is going on?" Gershom asks. Rosalind has been unable to keep up with the rapid exchanges.

"If you'd learn the language, Gershom, you'd be in the know," she snaps.

Gershom glares at her but doesn't say anything.

"Ladon, I will not lie to you," Sverre says.

"Who or what are Zzlo?" Rosalind asks.

"Slavers. They've haunted our history for generations. They are a force to be reckoned with."

"And they're here? Why? The planet is devastated—why are they here now?" Rosalind asks and looks to Calista, who reluctantly translates for Gershom.

"As to that, I don't know," Sverre replies.

"Because they're evil," Ladon says. "We have to be ready to fight them. We need to bring the city defenses on line."

"I'm not having any luck there," Amara replies.

"I understand that," Rosalind says. "What do they look like? What are their capabilities?"

Sverre reaches in front of him and taps the table with his finger. A panel slides aside then a console lights up in response. All of us look from it to him. His fingers clack on the keys then a hologram appears in the middle of the table. A space pirate. Just like the ones that attacked our colony ship and caused us to wreck.

"Son of a bitch," Amara mutters.

"Anyone else notice they look like a cross between a Predator and Reavers?" Mei asks.

I look at her, back at the hologram, then bust out laughing. "Man, you're right!"

Calista grins too but no one else seems to appreciate the joke, so I force myself to quit laughing. "Sorry."

"Those look like the ones who attacked our ship," Inga says.

"They are the same," Calista says.

"Hey look, Gershom, it's your uncle," Amara says.

Gershom's face turns purple and he splutters.

"Enough," Rosalind says.

Amara smiles, unapologetic, but doesn't say anything more.

"Where?" Ladon asks.

"A day and a half to the east," Sverre answers. "Their ship

is intact. They will find us sooner or later if they're looking. I don't know why else they would be here."

"What about the ones that crashed when we did?" Inga asks. "Calista mentioned running across one when her and Ladon came to help us."

"That could be what it is," Sverre says. "In that case they may leave without harassing us. There are not many of us and I doubt it would be profitable for them to gather those of us still here."

"We should prepare anyway," Ladon says.

"I agree, but we need to look at all we face and prioritize it," Sverre says.

"I agree," Rosalind says.

She and Sverre look at each other with deepening respect.

"I understand I've just arrived, so I do not know what has been done. I know that Jolie needs epis," he says this mostly to Ladon.

"We've farmed some, but our supplies have run out," Ladon says.

"You were able to farm it on your own? Impressive," Sverre says.

"It was young," Ladon says, brushing aside the compliment.

"Jolie will need it still, which is a priority," Sverre says.

"Defense is a priority," Rosalind says.

Sverre turns to face her full on. He doesn't say a word. The two of them stare at each other and silence falls across the table. Butterflies dance in my stomach watching him stand up to Rosalind, the Lady General, for me. A minute crawls past and still they stare at each other. Then, finally, Rosalind nods agreement.

"Thank you," Sverre says, bowing his head to her.

"We need to get those shields working," Rosalind says. "Amara can you report on your progress?"

"I'm at an impasse," she says. "As far as I can tell, they should be working."

"I believe I can assist in that, once we have epis for Jolie," Sverre says. "When we return, I will look into it."

"We can't wait for that!" Gershom cries out when Calista translates, jumping to his feet. "The shield is a priority over all."

"As much as I hate it, I have to agree with Gershom," Rosalind says. "You just warned of us of a new threat. One we are woefully unprepared to face. We need those shields."

Sverre stares down at the table in front of him his hands balled into fists. His jaw tightens. I place a hand over his fist. "Please help us get the shield up," I plead.

"Okay," he says. "I will do what I can to start the shield. Once that is done, we mount an expedition for epis without further delay."

"Agreed," Rosalind says and raps the table signaling the adjournment of the council meeting.

18

JOLIE

"There is a cavern nearby," Ladon says as most of the group files past us.

Calista is on his arm grinning while I'm on Sverre's arm doing the same back to her.

"Good, how dangerous is it?" Sverre asks.

"As you'd expect," Ladon says. "It's not unmanageable. It will be easier with another Zmaj."

"Do what you can to prepare," Sverre says.

Ladon hisses then he and Calista walk away. Amara is waiting a short distance off watching us. She walks up once they are gone.

"I want to help," she says.

Sverre stiffens. It's subtle and if I wasn't holding on to his arm, I might not notice.

"Thank you, this is something I must do on my own," he answers her.

Amara bites her lower lip while putting a hand on her hip. Jealousy stabs into my heart, watching her look at him with her pretty dark eyes.

"This is my area," she says, sounding petulant.

Sverre looks down at her and his tail increases its tempo of back and forth.

"I understand," he says.

Amara stares at him, waiting for him to change his mind. Sverre stands waiting too.

"Why?" Amara asks at last.

"I'm not sure if I can," he says. "Let me investigate first."

"Fine," she says leaving.

"So does that leave me out as well?" I ask, now that we're alone.

Sverre stares silently. The lash of his tail back and forth is enough to tell me he's upset. I stand in front of him and place a hand on his chest.

"Talk to me," I speak softly.

"Jolie," he says, his voice tight. "There are things I don't want to remember. Things I don't want to know. I know I did things. Doing this will bring them back."

"It's okay," I say. "We'll face them together."

His mouth tightens into a hard line, but he puts his hand over mine on his chest.

"Let's go," he says, slinging his pack over his shoulder.

He leads the way through the building and down into the depths. Amara has been working on the motors that are found down here. The motors are massive. Each one of them is as large as a small building in its own right and there are dozens of them, lined up in rows. We walk down the rows, and he doesn't look to either side. He keeps his gaze focused directly in front. Sverre walks in silence, and there's something so solemn about the moment that I can't think of anything to say either.

We reach a wall at the far end of the room and he stops. His head is bowed, his tail is moving back and forth quickly, and even his wings rustle like they have nervous energy running through them. He breathes deeply and closes his eyes.

"Sverre, what is it?" I ask as his breathing changes and becomes shallower.

"Memories," he exhales.

"Tell me," I whisper.

"No!" he cries, pulling back from me. "I can't."

Cold fear grips me, but this is Sverre. I know him and he is better than this. I know the man beyond whatever he's trying to confront. I won't let fear come between us.

"What?" I ask again, but I don't move any closer.

He shakes his head.

"It's all…"

I wait. Finally, I say, "All what, Sverre? What could be so bad? It's not going to change how I feel about you."

"Don't be so sure," he says, and the pain in his voice is enough to break my heart.

"How bad can it be?"

He shakes his head again. "I've done terrible things Jolie. I am undeserving of you. This is all a mistake. Once the shields are on, I will leave, you will find another. One worthy of a treasure such as you."

He pulls his bag in front of himself as he talks, reaches in, and pulls out the box that contains the shield thing. That thing, it's always at the center of his upset. What is it about that thing? He palms the shield, then closes his eyes and raises his hand to his chest and presses down. When he removes his hand, the shield remains in place. He steps back then up to the wall. Something grinds, then clicks. A green light shines from some point on the wall and moves up and down across the shield, and then the wall fades and is gone. A long walkway lies in front of us.

"Holy fading walls," I say, leaning into the new exposed area.

Sverre is still standing with his eyes closed, breathing in rapid gasps. I move in close to him until I'm pressed against the hard muscles of his chest. Putting my arms around his neck, I rise up on my toes until our lips meet. He doesn't resist but, for a moment, he doesn't respond either. I keep my lips pressed to his until at last he stirs. I'm pulling him from the fog of memory, away from his past.

"Sverre," I whisper his name.

"Jolie," he says.

"It doesn't matter," I say.

"You don't know," he replies. "I'm not worthy."

"I do know. You are," I say with all my heart.

Remembering suffuses his face. While he's looking at me, a part of him is looking at the past. I hold tight to him, anchoring him to the now, but it's all I can do. I feel him pulling away from me, even though he doesn't move an inch. The connection between the two of us is straining as he retreats.

"No, I was wrong. So wrong," he whispers.

"Talk to me Sverre, please."

His fabulous turquoise eyes bore into mine unblinking.

"You deserve to know," he says at last. "They all do. I'm no leader—I don't deserve to be around other people. I should return to my exile."

"Why?"

"It's my fault," he says, pulling out of my embrace.

I stare after him, my feelings hurt at his retreat. He turns his back on me but doesn't go any further.

"What are you talking about?"

"The devastation, the war, the destruction—it's my fault!" he says.

"What? How?"

He glances over his shoulder at me and I realize how

141

harsh my voice must have sounded. I didn't mean for it to, but I was surprised by what he said.

"Because I pushed the vote, I let it come to the table."

"Sverre, what are you talking about? What does this have to do with that Star Trek looking thing on your chest, and what does any of this have to do with what happened? You're not making sense!"

"Aren't I?" he hisses, and suddenly he's angry. It pulses between us.

His hands close into fists and he whirls to face me. I take an involuntary step backwards more in surprise than anything else. His tail lashes and his wings flutter. He clenches his fists repeatedly until he seems to at last be in control of himself.

"Talk to me, please," I say and, despite the quaver of fear that chases its way down my spine, I walk to him.

Putting both my hands on his chest, I look into his eyes, and I stand before him waiting. He shakes his head, then like a balloon deflating, the anger drains out of him. The tension is gone and there's only the two of us standing together.

"You won't understand, how can you?"

"Try me," I say.

He closes his eyes, inhales deeply, and then begins.

"I was a leader of my people," he says. "I was Chair of the Ruling Council when we voted to rebel. The memory of it is vague—the bijass eats at the details—but I remember, so clearly, picking up the gavel and bringing it down. The rebellion would happen. My vote started it. I slammed the gavel."

"You couldn't have known," I say.

"It was my job to know," he says.

"Sure," I say. "You couldn't though. You just said yourself that the bijass eats at the details. How much do you really remember? How much do you know, and how much are you guessing?"

He shakes his head so I press forward.

"You're claiming it's all you but you said you were Chair of a Ruling Council, right? Then there were more than just you. How many? Five, ten, a dozen?"

"Fifty-seven," he says.

I stop and blink. "Fifty-seven?"

"Yes, one for each territory," he says.

"Oh," I say thinking that over. "So how could it ALL be your fault?"

"It was, my vote was final. I started the war that became the end of my race."

"Okay," I say.

"Okay?" he asks.

"Yes, okay."

"I don't understand," he says.

"I get it. It happened. You made a bad choice, and it went terribly. You can't change what happened then; you can only fix now, and you know what? We need you. Right now, your people need you. My people need you. What I saw in that room up there, that was a leader. Even big bad Ladon was listening to you."

"I'm not a leader," he says.

"Bullshit, you're like the Captain Picard of the planet!"

"Captain Picard?" he asks, confused.

"Never mind that, my point stands. You're the one we need. So, you screwed up. I still love you."

"Love?" he asks and everything stops.

The entire universe makes a clank sound as it comes to a screeching halt. I said it. The thoughts and feelings that have been growing inside my heart since I met him just blurted out. The word hangs between the two of us and I know it's going to crash down at any moment. As soon as the universe returns to motion, it will fall and everything will shatter. If I let it. I'm not going to because I realize now it's true. I'm in love with him.

"Yes damn it, I love you. And I'm pretty sure you love me too," I say with a confidence that feels like it's built on quicksand. One wrong word from him and my glass houses will shatter.

He stares at me, lights dancing in his beautiful eyes, then he moves so fast I barely see it happen. He's standing apart one moment then I'm off my feet and in his arms, swinging in a circle. He pulls me in tight, and then his wings pop out and wrap around the two of us as we kiss. His tongue seeks mine insistently until our kiss becomes a fuel for our passion. I can feel his arousal pressing into my abdomen as he continues to squeeze me tighter. We break the kiss to gasp in air, and I laugh. Then he's laughing, too.

"I love you," he says, his eyes sparkling.

I'm so happy that a tear slides down my face. He sets me back on my feet, then wipes the tear.

"I'm fine," I say, wiping at the next tear that tries to escape. "It's nothing."

"You are not sad?" he asks. "Or hurt?"

"No, I'm just... I'm so happy," I say, and then more tears are falling while I laugh.

"Happy," he says shaking his head. "Your race is very... inefficient."

"Yeah," I laugh. "I guess we are."

I lean against him and listen to the beating of his heart. It echoes which I've noticed before. It must be part of his alien biology.

"I am glad you have chosen me, Jolie," he says. "I knew, the moment I saw you, that you were the one for me. I did not want to force that choice on you. I wanted you to make it of your own free will. You make me very happy."

"You're so sweet," I say.

"Maybe in time we can discuss having children?" he asks.

I hadn't thought that far ahead, myself, but then I remember him miming something about my belly, and it hits me that's probably what he was trying to communicate.

"Oh," I say. "Yeah. I mean, I want kids. I do, but let's take care of everything else first, okay?"

"Of course," he says. "Let us activate the shield."

He keeps one arm around my shoulders as we walk through the disappearing wall. It leads us out onto a catwalk that drops into a black abyss on either side. It's designed for Zmaj to walk two abreast I would guess so there's no problem for the two of us to walk side by side. An eerie, oppressive silence sits in this room. Looking up I can't see a ceiling and there are no walls visible to either side. It's like walking a catwalk across nothing, through nothing, and to nothing.

I don't know how long we walk until there's a wall in front of us. Sverre walks up to it and touches something. A green light again beams out and scans his badge then the wall turns into some kind of touch-screen-like device. He works quickly, touching random symbols that cause other ones to appear. The machine that taught me to speak and understand his language does not seem to have imparted an understanding of the writing.

"Yes," he hisses then something clicks and there's a loud clang.

The sound of air flowing follows the clang then something whirs. The hair on my arms stands on end as the room becomes charged with static electricity. The blackness that surrounded us lightens until it's a dim gloom but not nearly as oppressive as it was. Sverre looks around then does some more things on the monitor.

"It is done," he says.

"Really? Let's go see it! I've got odds on this place looking like Gallifrey!"

"What is Gallifrey?" he asks as I pull on his arm trying to make him move faster.

"Sverre, I've got so much to teach you," I say, thinking of all the pop culture I need to bring him up to speed on. "But for now, hurry up! I want to see it!"

He smiles and then we run hand in hand.

19

SVERRE

"Oh Sverre, it's beautiful!" Jolie exclaims.

I pull her tight against me. The joy in her is infectious. "It is, isn't it?" I observe.

"We have to see it from higher, oh I want to see it from one of the dunes outside! It's amazing. I have to know if it looks like Gallifrey. I'm sure it does! The red sand and the sky, oh the domes will sparkle, the towers, it's got to be perfect!"

"How about we hold off on that?" I ask.

"Why?"

"I want to get the expedition for the epis organized for tomorrow. That will put us outside the city and we can see it all then."

Her shoulders slump but she nods agreement. "Fine," she says exaggerating being dejected. "If you insist."

Everything feels... good. Standing on top of one of the tallest buildings in the city and looking out I can ignore the destruction below us. The broken windows, the twisted steel, the hulking, rusted remains of vehicles and things that were. The domes sparkle, reflecting back the harsh sun and blocking out the worst of the heat. I don't mind, but I know it's hard on Jolie and any of her kind that haven't taken the epis yet.

Epis. The rise and fall of this planet, of my entire race, is told through epis. Once we numbered in the millions. Before the devastation, before my choice that changed our future. Melancholy comes through the fog of what was. How much of this is because I don't want to remember? How much is the bijass?

"Hey," Jolie says, pushing against me and pulling me out of my thoughts.

"Hmm?" I ask, tearing my gaze away from the horizon.

"Here, with me, right? Don't go getting lost in the past," she says.

"Yes, of course, my love," I say.

"I mean it," she says, rising on her toes and kissing me.

Wrapping my arms around her, it's easy to focus on the now. The way she fits against me, the taste of her sweet lips, the curve of her hips—all anchor me here. Where I should be.

Pulling away, I observe Jolie's eyes are sunken, her skin has a lack of tension to it. No matter how soft and sweet they are, the imprint of my lips on hers lingers. She's in a state of extreme dehydration.

"I need to find Ladon," I say. "We need the epis, today."

"Are you sure?" she asks. "Can't you let him go?"

I shake my head. "No, it is too dangerous for any one man."

"He's done it before," she says.

"He encountered a young one by his own words, and you yourself said he was injured. If he was to encounter a full-grown zemlja," I don't need to say more because she nods understanding.

"That's what I'm worried about," she places her hands on my chest.

Warmth blossoms under her touch and my body responds, my cock stirring, but now is not the time. I want her, badly, so instead I lean in and kiss her before taking her hand and leading the way back to street level.

"I want to go with you," she says.

"No," I reply.

"You know that's not going to work right?"

"I can try," I say.

"Okay, how about this? Let's short-circuit the entire thing. You say no, I say yes, we argue. I pout and stomp my foot. I'll be particularly petulant. Hell, I'll even throw some tears in there, and in the end, you will agree to let me come along. So can we just skip to the end?" she asks, grinning.

Going over her argument, I look for any flaw in her logic. Anything, any way I can prove her to be incorrect but nothing comes to mind. I close my eyes and shake my head.

"Will you agree to listen to me? Whatever I tell you, will you do it, without question?"

"Sounds kinky," she says.

"What is kinky?" I ask. "I don't understand how you're using that term, there is nothing curling about my words."

Jolie laughs. I love her laugh even if it is apparently at my own expense. Her voice is musical but her laugh is like a complex symphony of sounds creating a single crescendo that gives my soul wings and lets it soar.

"Um, I'll try to explain that later," she says. "It means, uh, non-standard sex?"

"Is there a standard for sex in your culture?"

"Uh, well, maybe? Crap, we're getting in deep now," she laughs, as her face turns a shade of pink.

"Deep in what?"

"How about, later, I show you some things?" she says with a grin, her face deepening to red.

"If it's with you, I'm all in."

149

She snorts and we walk into the main building, where I hope Ladon will be. He's walking through the lobby as we enter, with Calista and Rosalind at his side.

"Good morning," I greet them.

Ladon stares and tenses but retains control of himself. After a moment, he nods.

"I've got a few good men ready to go," Rosalind says.

"Good," I say.

"I'm going too," Calista says.

"No," Ladon retorts instantly.

All of us look at Calista who is far along in pregnancy by the looks of her swollen belly. While I agree with Ladon, I'm not sure I want to get involved. I've lost this argument already with Jolie.

"Absolutely not," Rosalind says. "You're getting too big and won't be able to move quickly."

"I can too!" Calista exclaims.

"It's not up for discussion," Rosalind says.

"They're probably right," Jolie says, taking Calista's hands in hers.

Calista's lips purse, and it's obvious she wants to argue.

"Fine," she says. "You bring my man home."

She looks at me when she says it. I nod, accepting the responsibility.

"Let's go then," Rosalind says, walking past us and out the door.

Outside, four more men have gathered. They carry with them metal barrels that I assume are weapons. They look similar to the ones I saw the Zzlo carrying. I wonder if they'll be effective against the armor of a zemlja but we'll find out in time. Touching my lochaber, I catch Ladon's eyes and glance at the weapons the others are carrying. He shrugs, so I assume he knows as much as I do about their use.

Ladon takes the lead and Rosalind walks beside him. We

follow two by two, Jolie and I next and the others behind. When we reach the access tunnel to exit the shield, Ladon stops and turns to me. I step up and touch my symbol to the control panel. The outer door disappears and we walk out into the desert.

Ladon once more assumes the lead since this is his territory. The sun rises as we walk, and I make sure that Jolie is drinking often. She adds a powdered supplement to her water that seems to help, and she takes some small white tablets. It's past noon when Ladon holds up a fist.

"Are we close?" I ask, keeping my voice soft.

He points to a dune. When I close my protective lenses, I can see a dark crack. Ladon resumes walking and now no one speaks. The men with us bring their weapons to the ready. The temperature drop is immediate when we enter the shadowy cavern, and it's welcome to Jolie, I'm sure. It causes a shiver to run down my spine as my body temperature drops to match it.

The cavern is large and open. The ceiling is dozens of feet above us and the walls are distant. There is no epis in sight but that is to be expected. This opening is natural, not made by a zemlja so the required fertilizer would not be here for epis to grow. At the back of the cavern is a crevasse towards which Ladon is leading us.

Ladon presses himself into the rock. He has to turn sideways and is barely able to pass through. He's a ways in when the ground trembles and he freezes.

"What the hell?" one of the men behind me mutters.

I whirl around and slam my hand quickly over his mouth. His eyes widen and he raises his weapon between us. The other men bring their weapons noisily to bear on me but I shake my head furiously, holding my fingers over my own mouth. He nods behind my hand and I remove it, but the ground is still trembling. Dust and small rocks fall from overhead, raining down on us. It's coming closer. The man who spoke is shaking, his face turns pale, and he's looking around with wide eyes. The moisture on his face is pouring out, dripping off of his chin as he starts turning from side to side, his weapon rattling with each movement.

I shake my head trying to get his attention, trying, silently, to make him stop, but he's not paying attention. The tremble becomes a rumble and larger rocks fall from above us. A slide happens on the far wall as a section of it crumbles, falling loudly to the ground. The man shakes his head, raising his weapon towards the slide, then the thing in his hands barks wildly. The sound of it is deafening.

I tackle the man, dragging him to the ground. The weapon keeps barking until we hit the ground when it stops at last. I hold him still despite his struggling. I'm larger and stronger than he is, but it's too late. The rumble grows louder still. The zemlja has tracked its prey. Our only hope now is to run. We'll have to fight it, but not here where we're confined by the cave.

"Out!" I yell, looking over my shoulder and spotting Jolie.

She runs, obeying me without question. Good girl. The others move along with her. Rosalind stays behind, yelling and pointing in her own tongue. Ladon is exiting the crevasse, but the ground is bucking as the zemlja gets closer. He's almost out when I see the walls to either side shift and he cries out in pain.

"Ladon!" I scream, climbing off the man I'd been restraining.

"Get out of here," Ladon barks.

Ignoring him, I grab his hand and pull. He's stuck tight and I gain no headway. Placing a foot against the wall, I pull again but he grunts in pain. The strain on his shoulder is too much. The ground is bucking up and down, making the opening tighter.

"I can't leave you behind," I say, stepping back and crouching down to be jarred less while I survey the situation.

"Stay and we both die," he says. "Get out of here, survive, and take care of Calista and my child."

"No, I promised her I'd bring you home," I say. "I won't let my people down again."

The rocks shift and then I get an idea.

"You're being stupid," Ladon grunts.

"Spread your wings, warrior," I order.

"I can't," he says.

"You can, you must! Spread them, it will ease the pressure, but you have to do it now."

He cries out in pain, but his wings spread out and I take his arm and pull. He pops out of the crevasse and we fall to the ground, with him landing on top of me. He leaps to his feet, takes my arm, and pulls me up. Together we run out, the last to exit from the cavern.

"Sverre!" Jolie screams, seeing me, and starts running.

The ground between the two of us explodes. Sand and rocks fly upwards obscuring my view of her. Behind the exploding earth comes the zemlja. I'm knocked backwards by the force of its eruption.

"JOLIE!" I scream.

I'm tumbling head over heels. I slam into the ground hard and something breaks in my chest. I feel the crack, a stabbing pain, and then a numbing sensation spreads. Climbing to my feet, I waver, then steady myself. I reach for my lochaber but my hand comes up empty. Twenty feet in front of me, it sticks up out of the sand like a marker. On the far side of it, another thirty feet, is the zemlja. It's massive, forty feet around at least, rising twenty-five feet into the air. The earth-dragon is the most fearsome thing on the planet and this one is fully grown.

It waves back and forth, snapping its maw. The body of a

zemlja is round, supple, and long. They travel under the earth, digging tunnels as they inch their bodies along. They're meat eaters that hunt by sound. Anything along the surface is in danger as they dig up from below and catch their prey unaware.

They're also the source of the epis, which is fertilized by their excrement. The zemlja's body is covered with a shell-like carapace that layers one over another to protect it from any other predator. Jolie is on the opposite side of this one, which means I need its attention to be on me. Away from her.

"ZEMLJA!" I scream to attract its attention.

It waves back and forth then locks on to the sound of my voice. It turns its mouth towards me and I run forward, hoping to close with my lochaber before it decides to slam down and crush me. My fingers are almost close enough to grasp the hilt of my weapon.

"ROLL!" Ladon screams from behind me, and I do so without thinking.

Tucking my head and pulling my tail and wings tight, I shoulder roll to the left and keep rolling, hoping I can make enough distance to escape the slamming worm.

It hits the ground and I'm thrown airborne again, still in a tight ball. My ribs scream from the position and it's almost impossible to catch my breath. When I hit the ground, I'm dazed. I can't clear my thoughts or take in enough air. Everything spins and all I can think of is Jolie. The sweet sound of her voice calling my name. Jolie, she's in danger. I have to save her. I stand up, pushing past the pain, past the confusion. None of that matters. Jolie needs me.

Stars dance at the edge of my vision. Every time I blink, the scene before me blurs, then comes clear, then blurs again. The zemlja is rising back up into the air. People are screaming. There is an incessant barking sound followed by pinging. The men that came with us are using their weapons, but as I thought, they are ineffective against the zemlja. The projectiles they send at it are bouncing harmlessly off its scales, but they continue trying as if it might change. Fools.

Ladon has his lochaber and is standing in front of the zemlja. I have to help him. My lochaber is still sticking out of the ground where I spotted it before, but now it's dozens of yards away. I have to reach it to help him, to save Jolie. Where is she? I run for the lochaber, looking for her as I do. There! I spot her behind the men with their weapons. She sees me running and screams my name.

"RUN!" I yell at her pointing towards the city. "NOW!"

I know she's going to argue, disobey, but I can't spare any more attention. I hope she listens. A shadow falls across me as I run. I glance up just in time to see the zemlja slamming down. I tuck and roll, this time keeping my sense of direction and aiming for my lochaber. When it hits, I'm thrown up but I'm in control now. I uncurl and spread my wings, gliding to a stop next to my weapon, which I grab. I whirl to face the monster.

I can't see Ladon. I hope he's alive. I can't do this alone. A zemlja has three weaknesses. The eyes, located at the top of its head, very difficult to reach due to its size alone. The mouth, filled with acidic spit and rows of razor sharp teeth, and the last place you want to be close to. Lastly the overlap of the scales. The lochaber is designed so that you can slide the blade between the plates. If you hit something sensitive, you can kill it.

The eyes are my best bet on one this size. In order to reach its eyes, I have to climb up on it and hope it doesn't dive below the earth before I reach them. Where is Jolie? Looking as I run for the monster, I see her watching. She didn't run, damn it. I told her to obey me no matter what, and she's still there behind the other men. They've stopped using their weapons, realizing at last that they're ineffective. Rosalind has drawn a thin sword and is running for the beast just as I am.

Rocks strew the path in front of me and I leap up them gaining momentum. I target a large one as I leap from one to another reaching the biggest one that is closest to the beast. Leaping from it, I spread my wings and strain with all I've got, gaining height as I soar through the air for the zemlja.

"Sverre!" I hear Jolie scream but I can't spare even a glance in her direction.

If this doesn't work, I hope she knows I did this for her.

The zemlja moves back and forth. I'm ten feet below its maw when my feet touch its scales. I'm sliding down the side of it. Whirling my lochaber I grip it with two hands and thrust between two of the scales, driving it into the tender flesh. It catches and I use it to stop my slide. The zemlja screams, an ear-shattering sound. I shake my head to clear it, then move up the haft of my lochaber hand over hand.

Climbing up towards the worm's back, I see motion on the other side. Ladon and I arrive on top of the beast at the same time. Exchanging a brief nod, I brace myself with my feet while grabbing an overlapping scale with my left hand. Using my right, I jerk my lochaber free, stretch as far as I can, and drive it between two scales.

The zemlja screams again and something pops inside my ears, causing an explosion of pain that blinds me for an instant. My sense of balance is gone. Dizziness rocks through me and I'm in motion, causing even more confusion. I grip tight to my weapon, knowing that an impact must be coming. It hits, and I'm bucked up off the zemlja, then slammed back down against it. Already-broken bones stab deep inside my chest. Breathing becomes a labored affair, but I can't let that stop me. Jolie is still too close. This thing must die. It will not harm her.

A few more feet. Only a few more feet and I will reach its eyes. Once more I clench a scale, free my lochaber, and then drive it in. I'm close to its head now. Ladon is beside me but we don't spare time for each other. The thing rises back into the sky, straight up, I'm dangling by my grip on a scale and the haft of my lochaber. It takes all my will to hang on despite the pain, the inability to breathe, the dizziness—all conspire, pushing me to let go, to give up. Jolie swims in my vision and I find the strength in her to hang on.

It's moving, waving, and I'm able to get my feet back on. I don't bother with the lochaber. The ridge of bone surrounding its eye is just beyond my reach. Bracing, I leap for it, spreading my wings and driving myself up. My fingers brush it and I start to fall, but I push my wings harder and gain an inch, then my fingers close on it. I'm hanging by one hand as it shifts and I lose my footing again. Straining, I pull myself up. Every part of my body screams in pain. It's too much but I can't give in.

"JOLIE!" I scream.

A force from below propels me the last few precious inches up and I'm there! Ladon used his own body to help me reach the worm's weakness.

I draw my knife with my free hand, and as my head comes up over the top of the zemlja, I drive the dagger into its eye with all the force I can muster. Its massive maw opens, screams, and row upon row of razor sharp teeth smash together. I push down with all I have, driving the dagger in deeper, trying to reach the brain behind the eye.

Wind rushes past as blackness closes in. Stars dance in the blackness and my last thought is of Jolie.

"I love you, Jolie," I whisper as the blackness claims me.

20

JOLIE

"*B*e okay. Please be okay," I whisper over his still form.

None of us are familiar with Zmaj physiology so our treatment has been a guess and a hope. I've been sitting here at Sverre's side for the past thirty hours. Waiting. Hoping. Praying.

I hear the door open and the approach of soft footsteps. A hand grips my shoulder, and Calista rests her head against mine. I put my hand on hers and a tear slides down my face.

"He'll be okay," she says reassuringly.

Sverre's chest rises and falls with shallow, short breaths.

"He has to be," I say my voice choking. "He saved us."

"Ladon agrees. He says he's never followed a braver man into battle."

A smile plays at the corner of my mouth but it can't overcome the weight of my worry.

"Why doesn't he wake up?" I ask, my voice soft as it passes the lump in my throat.

"He's healing, Jolie," Calista says. "A rib punctured his lung, three other ribs were broken, his wing was damaged, and he fractured his wrist. Once his body catches up, he'll wake. There's no signs of any brain trauma."

"I know. I just… It's been so long," I say.

"I know," she agrees.

She pulls a chair over and sits down close enough so that she can put an arm around my shoulders. I lean over against her and some of the weight on me seems to lift.

"I don't want to be here without him. I can't imagine a world in which he's not by my side."

"You won't have to," she promises.

We sit in silence with nothing more to say. An hour passes. I notice that he's breathing deeper and with less effort. His tail shifts as he takes a deep breath.

"JOLIE!" Sverre yells, sitting straight up in bed. His arms flail out wildly.

"I'm here, it's over!" I cry out throwing myself into his arms.

He wraps them around me, pulling me tight, and cradles me against his chest while getting his bearings.

"You are not hurt?" he asks, and I look up into his eyes.

"I'm fine," I say, tears streaming down my face.

"She is fine?" he asks Calista, apparently not believing me.

"She's fine. It's you we've been worried about," Calista says.

He nods. He takes a deep breath and I see him wince.

"I'm fine," he says. "The zemlja? Ladon? Did we harvest the epis?"

"Everyone's fine," I answer him. "And yes, we got the epis."

"You took it? You must take it," he says inspecting me.

"Yes," I smile at him.

He nods satisfied then takes another deep breath. He grimaces showing it obviously hurts but it must be better than it was because he follows it with another.

"Ladon is fine?" he asks.

"Yes," Calista says. "He was bruised and he strained his left wing, but he's fine."

"Good," he says.

"Are you okay?" Calista asks.

"I'm fine," he says dismissively.

"Right," she says. "Are you really okay?"

I sit up from him and he looks from her to me and then nods.

"Yes, there is pain; some ribs are broken but healing. My wrist hurts and my wings are strained. A few days and I'll be fine."

"Good," Calista says. "I think I'll leave you two alone for a bit then."

She smiles and leaves the room. I stand up and follow her out, thanking her for everything she's done. I shut the door and then stand with my hand on it before turning around.

"That was the dumbest, stupidest, damnedest thing I've ever seen, and don't you ever do that again," I say, stalking towards him.

He has the decency not to argue. Sverre hangs his head.

"I agree," he says. "It had to be done, though. Those men with their weapons would have attracted its attention, which would have brought it towards you. I had to save you."

"I was fine," I say.

"No, you weren't," he says simply.

"You scared me," I admit the truth behind my righteous anger. "I thought I was going to lose you."

He touches my cheek, trailing his fingers along my jaw.

"I don't want a world without you," he says, his beautiful turquoise eyes swimming with emotions.

My smile pulls the corners of my mouth up washing away the fear and anger and upset.

"I don't want one without you," I say, kissing him and letting everything else go.

Footsteps run down the hallway, a lot of them, breaking our kiss.

"What is that?" he asks.

"I don't know," I say as I walk to the door and look out.

A man assigned to be a guard is running down the hall.

"What's happening?" I yell at his retreating back.

He looks over his shoulder and yells back. "Intruders at the shield. Amara's outside."

"Damn it," Sverre says from behind me then he's right there.

"You're injured!" I exclaim.

"I said this would happen. Others are coming. If they're here, we need to reach them beyond the bijass. I need to be there. No one else understands this like I do."

"No, no way! You're still hurt."

He stares into my eyes, not arguing with words, but I feel him. I know what he's thinking, what he wants to say, and he knows what I want to say. Our understanding of each other is so complete that words aren't necessary. He's right and I know it, despite my fears of losing him or seeing him injured again. Giving in, I step to one side and follow him out the door. We run the same direction the guard was running, following the sound of his echoing footsteps until we're outside. Then it's a simple matter of following the crowd. Everyone is heading to see the action.

Dozens have gathered at the shield, blocking the view of what's going on. Sverre pushes through and they part around him like water. One of the multiple airlocks is here and on the other side are two Zmaj facing off with each other. A short distance on the far side of them is Amara, who is sitting on the side of a dune. Blood is trickling from under her hand that she's pressing to her forehead. The box I'd gone to investigate when all this started is close to her.

The two Zmaj circle each other with their weapons

drawn. One of them swings his in a slow, lazy circle, then drives in swinging it down in an overhand maneuver. The other blocks it and sparks fly as their blades meet with a ringing clash. Sverre activates the control panel then opens the door to the airlock. He enters it and I try to follow him, but he motions and the door closes, locking me out.

"SVERRE!" I yell at him angrily.

"Jolie," he shakes his head. "Please."

Everyone is watching the two of us when it hits me. He's a leader. Unlike Rosalind and Ladon, who are warriors, he's a leader we can follow. If people believe in him. I can't undermine that, and if I act like a petulant child, I will. Meaning to or not, I will undercut him in front of all these people. If they see him end this violence, then we're taking a step to a better future. My thoughts flash through in an instant then I nod my agreement. He smiles and touches the shield. I put my hand up against his and the shield sends a tingle through my body. The door on the opposite side opens, and he walks out.

"Brothers," he says without yelling.

The two Zmaj ignore him intent on killing each other.

"She is mine!" one of them yells.

"In death," the other responds, cutting low with his blade.

The first one dodges and bumps against Sverre. His tail lashes hard and Sverre has to jump up and back to avoid having his legs taken out from under him. He lands in a crouch and winces, one hand going to his ribs.

"Enough!" Sverre yells, rising up straight.

Something in his voice cuts through the rage of the two Zmaj. They stop, glaring at each other but no longer attacking. The one closes to Sverre hisses and the other shifts his grip on the haft of his weapon.

"She is mine," the one furthest from Sverre hisses. "I saw her first."

"Wrong," the other replies.

"She is neither of yours," Sverre says walking between the two of them. "She belongs only to one she chooses. You are not animals!"

Their attention is now on him. He stands unarmed between the two of them. My stomach ties itself into knots. I couldn't get to him in time to stop them cutting him down if I tried. No one can. He's made his play and if they don't listen, he's dead.

"Who are you to speak to me in such a manner," the one to the left hisses raising his lochaber.

"I am Sverre, formerly Head Chairman of Tajss. You are in the territory of Ladon of Drakonov. Come as a friend and be welcome. There are plenty of threats to be faced besides one another."

"Sverre," the right one hisses. "I do not recognize your authority."

"Your recognition does nothing to lessen my stance. This woman is under my protection."

"Then I will take her from you," the right one responds.

"No, she is mine!" the left one interjects.

Sverre reaches out to them both, moving slowly but confidently, he places a hand on each man's shoulder.

"Perhaps she will choose one of you," Sverre says. "You are men of honor, Zmaj. Tell me your names. Push past the grip of instinct, and remember who and what you are."

His touch changes them. They relax. The tension drains away and both men stand straighter.

"I am Shidan," right hand says.

"I'm Astarot," the left-hand man says.

I let out the breath I've been holding since he walked between them. The two Zmaj fall into conversation with Sverre. Shidan is tall, three or four inches taller than Sverre, putting him well over seven feet tall. His markings have red tinging his scales, and he has emerald eyes that sparkle in the light. Astarot is shorter than Sverre. His scales are tinged with a bright green that edges towards fluorescent, while his eyes are darker, dark brown or maybe even black—I can't tell for sure at this distance.

Sverre talks to them as he helps Amara to her feet. She appears fine, having a minor cut on her forehead. Sverre opens the airlock and ushers her in but remains outside with the two Zmaj. Finally, he turns to me.

"Can you go and get Ladon? I need him to welcome these two into the city."

It turns out to not be necessary because, as soon as I turn to ask the man next to me to run for him, I see Ladon striding down the street. He looks angry as he moves with determination towards the airlock.

"What is the meaning of this, Sverre?" he asks, not opening the door, and crossing his arms while staring at Sverre.

"Ladon," Sverre says. "We have visitors."

"I see this," Ladon hisses.

Rosalind pushes through the growing crowd to stand next to Ladon, followed by Calista. The two newcomers have their weapons in hand and ready. Sverre stands between them. People in the crowd behind me are muttering. Calls to keep them out, complaints about more aliens, and a minority who seem ready to welcome them in.

"Open the door," Rosalind says to Ladon.

"No," Ladon says, eyes locked with Sverre.

"I'm not asking," Rosalind says, and Ladon looks over, anger pulsing from him in palpable waves.

Sverre steps closer to the dome, which puts the two newcomers at his back.

"Everyone," he says looking at me. "Jolie can you translate for me?"

"Of course," I agree, my heart swelling as he transforms before me.

"The future lies before us," he says, and I translate. "The past, who and what we were, what we've done, doesn't matter. The survival of both our races has been intertwined. By fate, by gods, or by sheer luck I do not know. What is clear, abundantly, is we need each other."

The crowd shifts and mutters, but they're listening. Ladon drops his arms to his sides as his anger becomes less visible. Calista puts her arm around him. The two newcomers stare at Sverre, then Astarot puts his weapon away.

"It will not be easy. We, each of us, have our personal fears and worries to conquer. What I can tell you is that we face enough threats from outside. There is no need for us to make enemies of each other. The only way I see forward that has any hope for either of our races is together. We must form a new tribe, a single tribe, integrating our two races and cultures together to create a new and brighter future for our children."

"Finally!" someone in the crowd shouts.

"That new alien makes sense," someone else says but I can't see who.

"It's a damn trap, aliens are going to kill us all and eat us," someone mutters but another person yells for them to shut up.

Rosalind is watching the crowd, her lips pursed, then she nods.

"He's right," she says, adding her voice and the weight of her leadership to him. "If we're going to survive, we need each other."

"Ladon?" Sverre asks.

Calista rises onto her toes and whispers into Ladon's ear. As she settles back to her feet, they kiss, then he looks at

Sverre. He doesn't speak as he goes to the control panel for the airlock and opens the door. The crowd behind us cheers, though a few of them hiss and boo. The majority seem to get it, and I guess that's the best we can hope for.

Sverre comes in first, followed by the two newcomers. A new day is dawning for our races. It's not going to be easy, I'm sure, but we're moving in the right direction. Rosalind takes Amara, whisking her off for first aid, and I throw myself into Sverre's arms.

"You're amazing," I say before kissing him.

"No," he says simply. "I'm practical. We need all the help we can get. It's the sensible solution."

"Well, be that as it may, I think you're amazing and I love you."

"And I you," he says softly returning my kiss anew.

"It is time for change. Will you join me?"

21

JOLIE

m I ready for this?
I don't know. I guess the time for not being ready would have been before it happened. Now, well now it is what it is. And I'm happy about it. Nervous, sure, but happy. It's been almost two weeks since the other Zmaj arrived. Integration is progressing slowly. Some of the humans don't want the aliens and there's a growing faction centered around Gershom.

There have been isolated reports from scouts about traces of what might be the Zzlo but no further sightings. Life is still a day-to-day struggle for something more than just surviving even if we're making headway. Food is a major concern. Our supplies are getting lower and while Rosalind and Sverre are organizing hunting parties for bivo meat, that won't meet all our nutritional needs. Calista and I have to find some way that we can grow plants.

"Is the answer in that wall?" Calista asks and I jump.

"Huh?"

Calista smiles. "You've been staring at that wall for the past twenty minutes."

"Oh, crap, sorry, yeah I…"

I haven't told her yet. I haven't told anyone, not even Sverre. I don't know what I'm waiting for, maybe for it to all sink in? To make sure it's real?

"Got it, so what's up?" she asks, cutting through any excuses.

I swallow hard. I can't not tell her. Calista waits patiently while I pull my thoughts together. She's getting bigger, definitely showing. Staring at her growing stomach, I blurt it out.

"I'm pregnant."

"Oh, that's great!" she exclaims taking me into a tight embrace.

"Yeah," I say, holding tight to her as nerves create intense butterflies in my stomach.

"What does Sverre think?" she asks.

"I haven't told him," I reply. "I'm going to tonight."

"He'll be over the moon," she says.

"Yeah, he wants kids. We've talked about it."

"And we'll only be a couple months apart! Our kids will grow up together. We'll have parties—it's going to be great."

"It will be!"

"You should probably know something else," she says.

"What?"

"Well, I was telling Ladon when I expected our baby would be born and he was surprised. I guess a Zmaj pregnancy usually lasts well over a year."

"You've got to be kidding me! Holy crap, we're going to be pregnant for a year? I'm gonna be a whale," I laugh and rub my still flat stomach.

"It's going to be great," she repeats.

We settle in to work and the day passes. Sverre is in meetings all day today organizing and building support for our two races becoming a single tribe. It's a visionary idea but also the only way we're going to survive.

Calista and I make some headway towards solving our food issue, and at last the day is done. We hug goodbye for the day, and I go to the room Sverre and I call home. He's waiting for me.

"Hello," he says. He wraps his arms around me from behind, pulling my hips tight to him, and I can feel his enormous erection pressing against me.

"Miss me?" I tease.

"More than words," he says.

"I can tell," I laugh, swaying and teasing him more.

"Mmm," he moans pulling my hair aside and kissing along my neck down to my shoulder.

"Sverre," I whisper.

"Mmm?" He continues kissing his way up my neck.

My thoughts scatter under the gentle ministrations of his tongue and lips. I turn my head, our lips meet, and we kiss. My passion rises to meet his, and all other considerations are gone. Pressing my tongue past his lips, I lick his teeth searching for his.

His hands grip my hips, keeping me tight against him. His cock pressing into my ass pulses. Grinding against him, I push his erection harder into my backside. His hands move between my legs and, as they move across my mound, I groan.

"Jolie," he growls, as we press into each other.

His hand slides into my pants and cups me, placing pressure directly over my throbbing clit. He moves his hand up and down, building desire. I throw my arms over my head and clasp them around his neck, holding him close. He kisses my neck and collarbone while his hand moves in a circle. One finger slides through my delicate silken folds to find my clit. He circles around it, driving me wild. My hips buck involuntarily and I groan.

I turn in his arms so that I'm facing him. Rising up on my toes, I press my lips into his, stealing a long, passionate kiss. He squeezes my ass then his hands are roaming down my legs and up my back.

"Sverre," I gasp, breaking the kiss. "I have something to tell you."

"Yes, my love," he says between kisses along my cheek and neck.

He keeps kissing, so I take his face in my hands and pull until we're looking into each other's eyes.

"We're going to have a baby," I say.

His eyes widen, his mouth drops open, and then I'm twirling in a circle. I grip his shoulders as dizziness takes hold of me. His laughter surrounds me along with his strong arms.

"You're certain?" he asks, putting me back on my feet at last.

"Yes!" I exclaim.

"Oh my love," he says, pulling me tight against him and kissing me with a fiery passion. "A child…"

"Ours," I reply.

"There is so much to do," he says stepping back. "The city must be prepared. The new tribe must be stabilized. The city defenses have to be strengthened and food supplies, those will have to be the priority, but we'll need crews cleaning and repairing as well."

"Sverre." I interrupt his stream of thought and his eyes return to me. "There's time."

"Yes, you're right," he smiles, wrapping me in his arms once more.

His rigid cock crushes between us, driving into my abdomen. As we kiss, I reach down and stroke his length, then slide my hand inside his pants and tease it with my fingers.

Leaning my hips out, I undo his pants and let them drop to the floor so that I have full access to him. He grabs my shirt and pulls it over my head. I lower myself to my knees before him. His beautiful, ribbed cock points at me, quivering with his need.

"Remember when I said I'd show you what kinky meant?"

"Mmhmmm," he moans.

"Well, here's lesson one."

I trace the side of his cock from its beautiful swollen head down to the base. His fingers twine in my hair and he moans loudly. I trace my tongue underneath it then up the opposite side, trailing my tongue just below the ribbed ridges that line the top of his shaft.

"Jolie," he groans as I reach the head and trace the lines with my tongue, flicking it over the tip of the head to tease him to even greater heights of passion.

His hips rock back and forth as I repeat my actions. He's too big for me to take fully in my mouth, but I slide the head in and close my lips tight around it, sucking while teasing it with my tongue. He groans and drops of his seed cover my tongue. Looking up at him, I see his eyes are rolled back in his head. His grip in my hair tightens, and he groans softly as he struggles to maintain control. I don't ease up; I want him out of control.

Sucking harder, I move his cock in and out of my mouth, driving down to the first of the ridges along the top while lavishing the underside with attention from my tongue. Sucking in and out as I move up and down makes him groan louder. His legs tighten and he pulls his hips back.

"Jolie, slow," he cries out, but I work faster.

His cock engorges further in my mouth and still he maintains control, so I grab the base of his shaft with my hand and stroke, squeezing the unprotected delicate underside. He's beyond words, moaning and making sounds that increase in volume and frequency as I work.

Impossibly his cock grows bigger still, then jumps in my mouth. I slide down as far as I can, then his seed explodes into me. His cock pulses and quivers as I slide off then stand up. Before I can get fully to my feet he grabs me, lifts me to his lips, and we kiss with a fiery passion. As we do, I feel his first, now-soft cock, retreat and his second one rise to the occasion. Such are the advantages of being in love with an alien dragon man.

He rips my shirt off, passion blinding him to the fragile buttons. He lifts me up until my breasts are level with his mouth, and he takes my nipple into his mouth, lavishing it with his tongue. Shifting his grip as he works me into diamond hard points, he hooks his arm under my ass, pushing my pussy against his hard chest.

The strength he has is incredible. He holds me up like I'm nothing in his arms. Running my hands over his head, down across the bulging muscles of his shoulders, I feel wetness streaming out of me as desire floods my body. We move across our apartment and into our bedroom, where he gently lays me down onto our bed. His muscles move under my hands making me hotter still.

On the bed, he moves over me kissing everywhere. His hands and fingers move, and it's like he has four arms. He's touching and exploring everywhere at once. The smell of him, so exotic, so spicy, combines with the musky smell of sex as my pants are ripped from me, leaving me fully exposed.

He stops, looking me over, drinking me in with his eyes. With any other man, I'd feel self-conscious, but the way he looks at me, I feel loved, wanted, appreciated. He lowers his body over me, then holding himself up on his elbows, kisses between my breasts and down across my stomach. He stops just above my bellybutton and kisses a slow, soft circle.

"Our child," he whispers. "I will make the world a better place for you."

My heart swells until I think I'm going to burst. Love fills me for him and for our child like a glowing golden light. A tear falls down my cheek as the emotions I'm feeling become too strong to process. I've never been so happy in all my life.

He kisses across my belly button and down to the top of my opening. Probing with his tongue, he parts my folds with slow, deliberate strokes of his tongue until he finds my clit. He traces circles around my throbbing nub. I grab his head and pull, clawing to bring him in closer, drive him deeper.

"Sverre, please," I cry my need out to him.

He drives his tongue tight against my clit and then he slides a finger inside. My walls tighten on that finger as my orgasm explodes. My toes curl tight, my back arches, and I cry out a wordless scream. Slowly it passes, and he pulls back his tongue and finger, then climbs up across me. Reaching my lips, we kiss. His tongue drives into me as his finger just did, finding my tongue and dancing.

His cock is at my opening and I'm so ready for him to fill me, take me completely. His forward thrust is fast and unexpected. He knows I'm so wet I can take him fully without preamble. He drives in and my pussy expands fast, then clamps down on him. He screams my name.

Stopping with the head spreading me wide, he drives back in, filling me. I buck my hips up to meet him, wanting, needing more. He loses control then as well, and we make love with wild abandon. Our hips rise and fall, meeting each other over and over in a dance as old as time.

Time disappears; everything is driven by the advance and retreat as we come together. He thrusts deep, pulls out. The fire builds into a roaring inferno that consumes everything in its path leaving only our love in its wake. Our love is forged in the fires of passion, the throes of desire, becoming hardened steel with which we will reshape the world.

One final piston and then I'm gone into the throes of orgasm. My back arches, and every muscle tightens like taut wires. Stars fill my vision, and we cry out each other's name as we come. Spent, we collapse into each other's arms. We lie entwined on the bed, kissing gently, letting the final quakes of our orgasms pass.

My love and I will build a better world for our child. We will make an unstoppable force. Sverre will lead us into a brighter tomorrow.

The End

Keep reading for a special sneak peek at *Dragon's Love*, available now!

SNEAK PEEK AT DRAGON'S LOVE

I guess I'm one of the last survivors of the human race and I'm stranded on this hell of a desert alien planet. Sucks to be me.

Our ship crashed months ago and those of us left are struggling to survive the boiling heat in barbaric living conditions. The only reason we're not all dead is one of my friends got knocked up by a native alien and he lets us live in his ruined city. We should be grateful but a lot of the humans hate the dragons and the girls who mate with them.

The natives are huge, seven foot tall dragon-men with wings and tails and scales. Surly and overly protective, who needs that? Not me. Alien baby fever is the new in thing, but I'm not falling for the hype. I've always survived being alone and I don't need anyone to change that. Try telling that to Shidan, the most annoyingly persistent alien male around.

Thanks to the primitive nature of the destroyed planet, we have no idea what's happening when things go wrong with my friend's pregnancy. I'm sure I can salvage something from our crashed ship that will help, but to get there I'll have to leave the city's protection and go out in the sweltering heat where everything wants to kill me. The only way I'll survive is if Shidan comes too and he's made it clear he wants only one thing. Love.

AMARA

"I won't let anyone else get hurt," I whisper, trying to convince myself.

Climbing to my feet, I rinse my face in a bowl of water then go to my bunk. I slip out of my clothes and under the salvaged blanket, staring at the ceiling. His lips were soft. So much softer than I expected. And that flavor, exotic, enticing awakened a long buried and forgotten need. An itch I haven't scratched in a long time, even before the wreck and destruction of my entire world.

My nipples stiffen at the memory of Shidan's strong hands holding me. In that instant I knew I was helpless. I hated it, but then something in me reacted different. Part of me liked it. I could have let him have it. Let him be in control but I had to fight it. He could handle it. The rough cloth of my blanket shifts across the diamond points of my nipples sending a shudder down my spine.

I cover the left with my hand to protect it and heat flares in my breast at my touch. The memory of his body pressing hard against mine consumes my thoughts. The way he felt, his erection digging into my stomach. He felt huge, massive, and now I'm wondering what his cock looks like. What would it feel like if I let him slide it into me?

My free hand drifts down between my thighs. I'm soaking wet with desire. Using a light pressure I rub a slow circle over my clitoris while my other hand pinches my nipple making it even harder.

He's strong. I like that. He took control, and he took what he wanted and it felt so damn good. My fingers slide inside.

My back arches as I enter myself. I imagine it being him. Pinning me down, he slides into me. Fills me with his massive cock. My pussy spreads to take him in. Pushing my fingers in and out as I think of him entering me, my core tightens. My fingers graze my clit. My back arches as muscles clench. His spicy, exotic lips claim mine. The bruises on my wrists, the ache in my shoulders as he holds my hands over my head. The way he'd take me, make me his.

I fuck myself faster. My fingers drive in and out as my wetness covers them. Three fingers slide in.

Imagination takes over. He's lifts me up by my wrists and carries me to the bed by hooking a hand under my ass. He squeezes my cheeks pulling my ass open as one of his rough fingers caresses my wetness. My delicate lips part before his touch.

A shudder races through my body. Spreading my fingers I fill myself up and drag them out and up over my clit. Pinching my nipple with my free hand I tug and pull on it as my fingers move faster. The pressure in my core is building. I'm gasping in air as my desire winds tighter.

Throwing me on the bed he leans over. His larger size engulfs me as he lowers himself between my legs. His tongue is rough as he drags along my opening, tasting my sweet wetness. He drives his tongue through my silken folds and I'm carried away to a new place.

My fingers explore as I dream of his tongue. He's dominating but attentive, I know he will be. The attention to detail he shows when he thinks he's caring for me make him an amazing lover. As my core tightens, I can't wait any longer.

His massive cock pushes into my opening. He's big, bigger than anything I've ever had. He slides in slowly, letting me get used to his girth. Nerves alight, everything is on fire. My mind explodes as I'm driven over the edge. Every muscle tightens and knots up, my toes curl and I can't breathe. Awareness returns in a slow pass back to reality as I collapse on the bed and exhaustion hits me.

I shouldn't have kicked him out.

No, I did the right thing.

DRAGON'S LOVE IS AVAILABLE NOW!

ABOUT THE AUTHOR

USA Today Bestselling Author of fantasy and scifi romance, Miranda Martin's books feature larger than life heroes with out-of-this-world anatomy and smart heroines destined to save the world. As a little girl she would sneak off with her nose in a book, dreaming of magical realms. Today she brings those fantasies to life and adores every fan who chooses to live in them for a while.

She was born and raised in southern Virginia, but as a veteran she's traveled to places like Korea, Hawaii and good 'ole Texas. Now she's settled in Kansas, the heart of America, with her husband and daughters. Her favorite animals are dragons, unicorns and cats. If she's not writing, you can still find her tucked away somewhere with a warm blanket and her nose in a book.

Get in touch!
mirandamartinromance.com
miranda@mirandamartinromance.com